5. The *śd̲m·yn·f* is a form of the past tense, and is used in a similar way to *śd̲m·n·f*. It was originally ceremonial, and is especially used when the subject is a person to whom respect is due; e.g. *rdy·yn ḥm·f* "his majesty gave."

6. The future or *śd̲m·ẖr·f* tense is a rare form, occasionally used in descriptions, and sometimes to express a mild command, e.g. *d̲d·ẖr·k r·ś* "say thou to her." The future is also expressed by means of the auxiliary followed by and the infinitive, e.g. *yw·f r śd̲m* "he will hear."

7. The emphatic mood appears in the weak and duplicating verbs, in that they duplicate the second consonant of the root to lay special stress on the idea expressed by the verb. Thus *mrr·f* "he certainly loves," or "may he love," instead of *mry·f* "he loves." It is used in sentences of wish, condition, question, consequence, &c., and sometimes introduced by a conjunction. It is frequent only in the active *śd̲m·f*, but is also found in the passive, *śd̲m·tw·f*, e.g. *n-ꜥꜣ·t-n mrr·y św* "because I certainly love him." The emphatic mood occurs in the regular strong verbs also, although it cannot be satisfactorily seen on account of the absence of vowels. In the synopsis I have, therefore, given the form which is possible, and more symmetrical, as the model verb *śd̲m* is used throughout. Other forms could easily have been used, which would have shown the duplicating in a graphical manner, e.g. *mśd̲d̲·f* "he certainly hates," *dd·f* "he certainly gives," *yrr·f* "he certainly makes."

8. The predicative is an old and rare form, which has the ending *w*. This ending, however, is usually not written. The predicative does not take a suffix, and is followed either by a substantive or an independent pronoun. In it the duplicating verbs show the doubling, and the weak verbs usually omit the last weak

consonant. It is used only in negative sentences after the verbs *tm* and *ymy* "not to be," and usually has an active meaning, e.g. N N *rꜣ n tm wnm N* "charm for the not-to-be-eaten of N" ("charm that N be not eaten").

9. The imperative has no means of showing difference in gender, although as Coptic shows there was a difference in vocalization. The duplicating verbs show their doubling in the imperative. (See § 87.)

10. The infinitive may be used as a verb or as a noun. In strong verbs its form is that of the simple root (e.g. *śḏm*), and in duplicating verbs it doubles the last consonant, e.g. *mꜣꜣ* "to see." (See § 88.)

11. In all participles the root of the duplicating verbs shows the doubling, e.g. *mrr·w* "loving." Participles are used like both adjectives and nouns. (See § 89.)

12. The relatives are forms derived from the *śḏm·f* and *śḏm·n·f* and used like nouns. The prospective relative form has recently been demonstrated by Gunn, *Studies in Egyptian Syntax*. The duplicating verbs have the doubling of the last consonant. (See § 90.)

13. Most passives are distinguished by the ending *tw* before the suffix. The passive with *w* in the singular (e.g. *śḏm·w·f* "he is heard") has *y* in the plural. But *w* and *y* in this passive are rarely written, and it is difficult to distinguish it from the active, e.g. *mś n·k ḫrd·w ḫmt* "three children are born to thee." Duplicating verbs show the doubling.

14. The conditional stem, or the pseudo-participle is the old inflection of the verb. Its place has been taken by the *śḏm·f*. Its transitive-active use is not extant, except in the case of the verb *rḫ* "to know." The pseudo-participle is, therefore, always intransitive and passive, e.g. *ywʿ·kwy m nb* "I was rewarded with gold." (See § 94.)

§ 80. *Vocabulary.*

ḫrw "voice," *wꜣḏ* "to be green," *šsp* "to take," "receive," *sꜥḥ* "freedom," *wḏ* "to command," *ḫft* "to," "before," *nḥm* "to take away," *ḥtp* "to rest," "to set free," "to satisfy," *ẖr-ḥꜣ·t* "before," *ḏbꜣ* "to pay," *yꜣw·t* "office," *mky* (*mꜥky*) "to protect."

§ 81. *Exercises.*

* In old texts when the subject of verb in the simple stem is a noun or absolute pronoun, the stem may take the ending.

CHAPTER IX

The Conjugation of the Strong Verb

The Simple Stem

§ 82. *Simple Stem–Active–Indicative.*

Present Tense

śḏm·f

śḏm·y	"I hear"
śḏm·k	"thou hearest"
śḏm·ṯ	
śḏm·f	"he hears"
śḏm-ś	"she hears"
śḏm·n	"we hear"
śḏm·ṯn	"you hear"
śḏm·śn	"they hear"

śḏm·kꜣ·f

śḏm·kꜣ·y	"thus I hear"
śḏm·kꜣ·k	"thus thou hearest"
śḏm·kꜣ·ṯ	

śḏm·kꜣ·f “thus he hears”

śḏm·kꜣ·ś “thus she hears”

śḏm·kꜣ·n “thus we hear”

śḏm·kꜣ·ṯn “thus you hear”

śḏm·kꜣ·śn “thus they hear”

Past Tense

śḏm·n·f

śḏm·n·y “I heard”

śḏm·n·k “thou heardst”

&c.

śḏm·yn·f

śḏm·yn·y “then I heard”

śḏm·yn·k “then thou heardst”

&c.

Future Tense

śḏm·ḫr·f

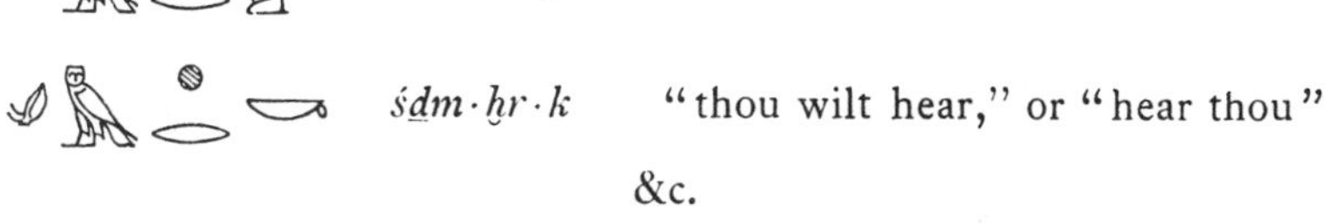

śḏm·ḫr·y “I shall hear

śḏm·ḫr·k “thou wilt hear,” or “hear thou”

&c.

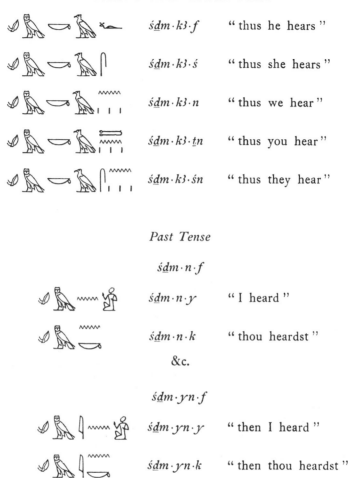

§ 83. *Simple Stem–Passive–Indicative.*

Present Tense

śd̲m·w·f or *śd̲m·tw·f*

śd̲m·w·y	"I am heard"
śd̲m·tw·y	
śd̲m·w·k	"thou art heard"
śd̲m·tw·k	

&c.

śd̲m·k3·tw·f

śd̲m·k3·tw·y	"thus I am heard"
śd̲m·k3·tw·k	"thus thou art heard"

&c.

Past Tense

śd̲m·w·f or *śd̲m·n·tw·f*

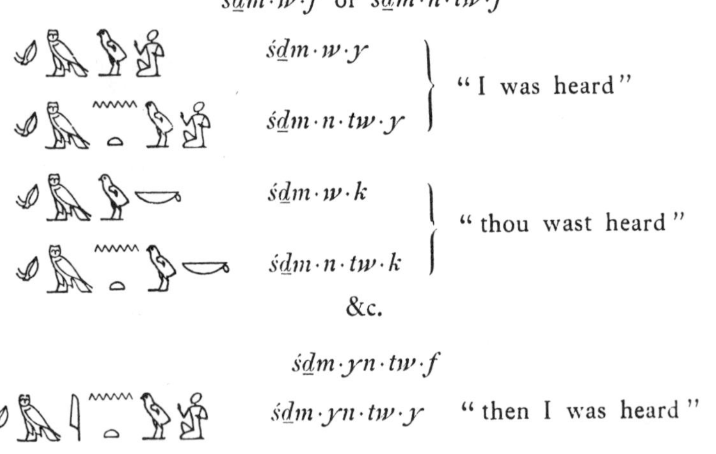

śd̲m·w·y	"I was heard"
śd̲m·n·tw·y	
śd̲m·w·k	"thou wast heard"
śd̲m·n·tw·k	

&c.

śd̲m·yn·tw·f

śd̲m·yn·tw·y	"then I was heard"
śd̲m·yn·tw·k	"then thou wast heard"

&c.

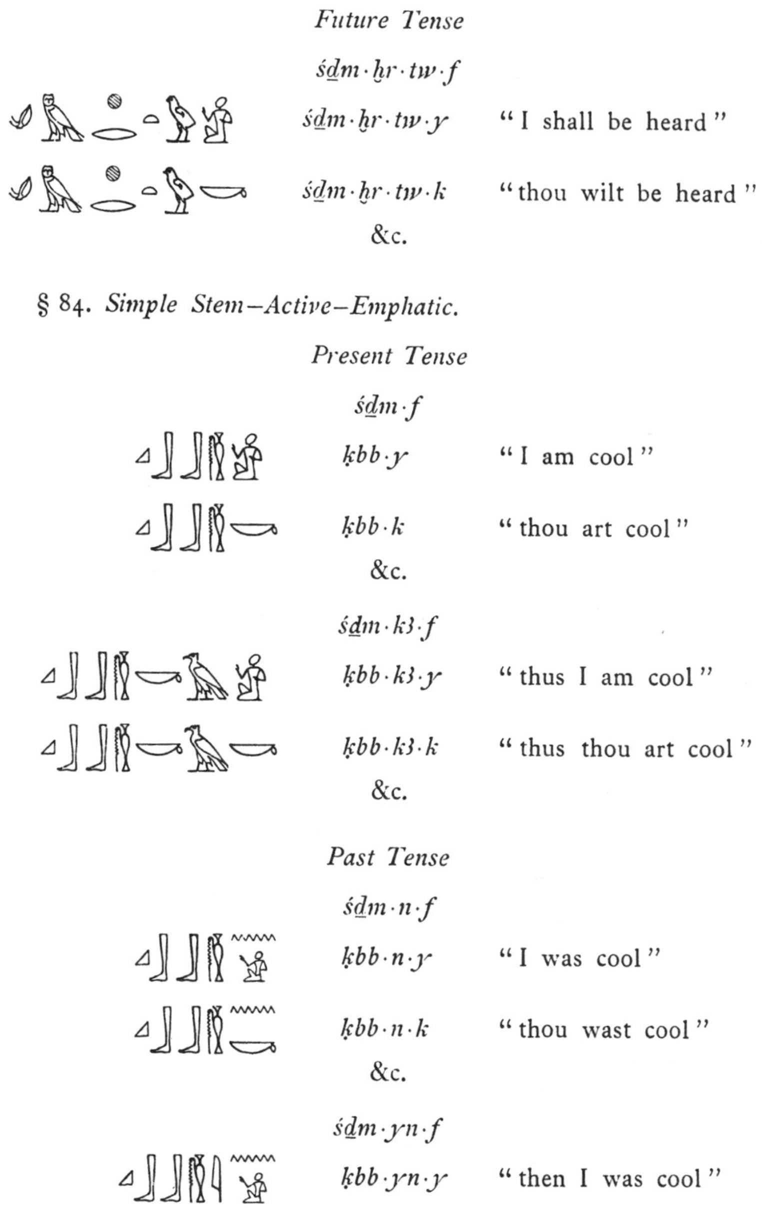

Future Tense

śḏm·ḫr·tw·f

	śḏm·ḫr·tw·y	"I shall be heard"
	śḏm·ḫr·tw·k	"thou wilt be heard"
	&c.	

§ 84. *Simple Stem–Active–Emphatic.*

Present Tense

śḏm·f

	ḳbb·y	"I am cool"
	ḳbb·k	"thou art cool"
	&c.	

śḏm·kꜣ·f

	ḳbb·kꜣ·y	"thus I am cool"
	ḳbb·kꜣ·k	"thus thou art cool"
	&c.	

Past Tense

śḏm·n·f

	ḳbb·n·y	"I was cool"
	ḳbb·n·k	"thou wast cool"
	&c.	

śḏm·yn·f

	ḳbb·yn·y	"then I was cool"
	ḳbb·yn·k	"then thou wast cool"
	&c.	

Future Tense

śḏm·ḫr·f

	ḳbb·ḫr·y	"I shall be cool"
	ḳbb·ḫr·k	"thou wilt be cool," or "be thou cool"

&c.

§ 85. *Simple Stem–Passive–Emphatic.*

Present Tense

śḏm·tw·f

	mꜣꜣ·tw·y	"I am seen"
	mꜣꜣ·tw·k	"thou art seen"

&c.

śḏm·kꜣ·tw·f

	mꜣꜣ·kꜣ·tw·y	"thus I am seen"
	mꜣꜣ·kꜣ·tw·k	"thus thou art seen"

&c.

Past Tense

śḏm·n·tw·f

	mꜣꜣ·n·tw·y	"I was seen"
	mꜣꜣ·n·tw·k	"thou wast seen"

&c.

śḏm·yn·tw·f

	mꜣꜣ·yn·tw·y	"then I was seen"
	mꜣꜣ·yn·tw·k	"then thou wast seen"

&c.

Future Tense

śḏm·ḫr·tw·f

m33·ḫr·tw·y	"I shall be seen"
m33·ḫr·tw·k	"thou wilt be seen"

&c.

§ 86. *Predicative.* For this form see § 79, 8.

§ 87. *Imperative.*

Strong Verb

śḏm	"hear thou"
śḏm·f	"let him hear"
śḏm·ś	"let her hear"
śḏm·y	"hear ye"
śḏm·śn	"let them hear"

Duplicating Verb

ḳbb	"be thou cool"
ḳbb·y	"be ye cool"

1. The imperative is strengthened either by an independent pronoun, by the particle , *yr*, or by the preposition , e.g. *ʿḥʿ yr·k* "stand up, thou," *šsp n·k ḥtp-nṯr* "take to thyself the divine offering."

2. The negative of the imperative is *ymy* "be not" with a following predicative, e.g. *ymy śnḏ* "fear not."

§ 88. *Infinitive.*

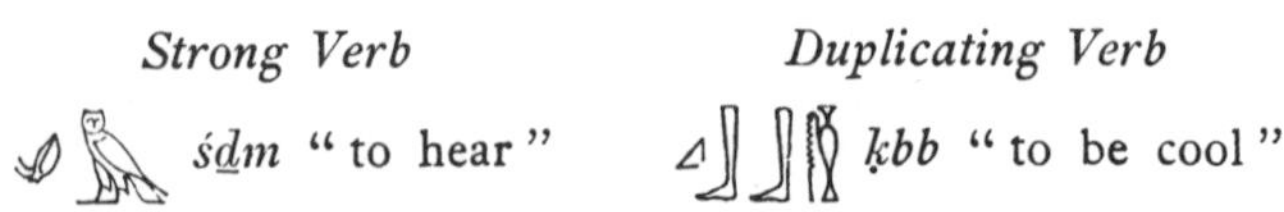

1. Weak verbs (see §§ 99 ff.) and the causative of verbs of two consonants take the feminine ending, e.g. *mśy·t* "to give birth to," *śmn·t* "to establish."

2. Uses of the infinitive:

a) As a noun, e.g. *nḥt·y pw yr·t n·f śt* "my wish it is to do it for him."

b) After verbs of commanding, willing, &c., e.g. *wḏ·n·f db3 śt* "he commanded to pay it."

c) After verbs of kindred meaning, as a complementary infinitive, to strengthen the idea expressed by the verb, e.g. *ḫnn·śn ḫn·t* "they rowed well" ("they rowed a rowing").

d) Governed by an adjective, e.g. *nfr mdw* "excellent (in) speaking" ("excellent to speak").

e) Used after prepositions, e.g. with to denote time, *m yy·t* "when they came"; with to express purpose, *r śḫr·t ḫftyw·f* "to overthrow his enemies"; with to express simultaneousness, *gm·n·f św ḥr pr·t* "he found him as he was going out"; with and to express cause, *mʿ yr·t m3ʿ·t* "because (I) wrought truth"; with *ḥnʿ* and a preceding verb, *yw·f ḥr wnm ḥnʿ śwry* "he eats and drinks."

f) Used in an explanatory clause, e.g. "she made it as her monument for her father Amon, *yr·t n·f tḫn·wy* making for him two obelisks."

g) There is a circumstantial form *śḏm·t·f* which has the appearance of a feminine infinitive, e.g. *pḥ·t·śn* "they arrived at" ("their arriving at"). It is used in a dependent clause, when the subject is different from the preceding clause, e.g. "I was astonished, *m yy·t·śn* when they came."

h) The logical subject introduced by or follows the infinitive, e.g. *dwꜣ Wśyr yn rpꜥ·ty* "worship of Osiris by the count."

i) If the object of an infinitive is a noun it follows immediately after the infinitive, but if it is a pronoun it is added to the infinitive as a suffix, e.g. *ḥr dwꜣ·f* "to adore him."

j) An infinitive may occur in successive sentences where we should expect a verb, e.g. *yr·t n·f śbꜣ m ynr* "and he made a door of stone for him."

§ 89. *Participle.*

The following forms apply to the perfect or imperfect, active or passive:

Strong Verb		*Duplicating Verb*	
Sing.		*Sing.*	
mas.	*śḏm*	mas.	*mꜣ*
fem.	*śḏm·t*	fem.	*mꜣ·t*
Plu.		*Plu.*	
mas.	*śḏmy·w*	mas.	*mꜣꜣ·w*
fem.	*śḏmy·wt*	fem.	*mꜣ·t*

1. The logical subject of passive participles is introduced either directly or by means of , e.g. *mry rꜥ* "beloved of Rꜥ," *mś n ḏḥwty* "created by Thot."

2. The rare participle *śḏm·n* "audible" indicates possibility.

§ 90. *Relatives.*

Strong Verb

śḏm·t·y "that which I hear"

śḏm·t·k "that which thou hearest"

&c.

Duplicating Verb

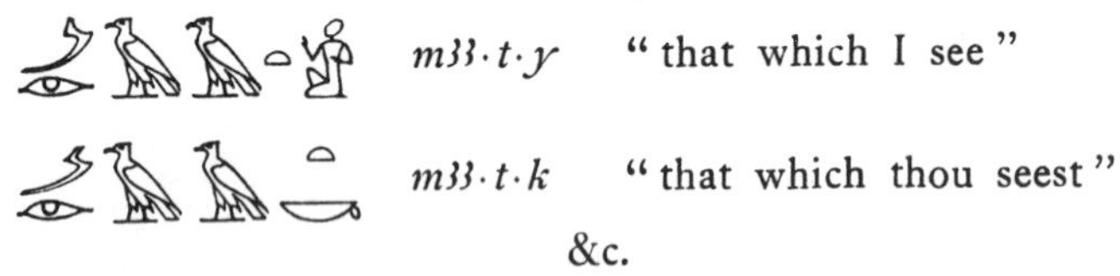

mꜣꜣ·t·y "that which I see"

mꜣꜣ·t·k "that which thou seest"

&c.

The relative forms usually introduce a relative sentence, e.g. *nfr yrr·t·y n·k* "that which I do to thee is good."

§ 91. *Verbal Adjectives.*

Verbal adjectives are really participles with a future meaning. The form is *śḏm·tyfy* "he who will hear." The root of a duplicating verb shows the doubling. Example, *m yꜣḫ·t n śḏm·tyfy* "as a splendid thing for him who will hear it."

§ 92. *Vocabulary.*

šmśy "to serve," "to follow," *ʿš* "to call," *ymy* "give," "put," *nṯr nfr* "good god" = "the king," *wr* "great," "to be great," *ḳny* "to be strong," *ẖrd* "child," *dw·t* "evil," *ḫnty* "to journey southward," *yny* "to bring," *wꜣ·t* "way," "road," *rd* "leg," "foot," *ynb* "wall," *ẖr* "under," "with," *hrw* "to be content."

§ 93. *Exercises.*

CHAPTER X

The Conjugation of the Strong Verb (*Continued*)

The Conditional, Causative, and other Stems

§ 94. *The Conditional Stem (Qualitative or Pseudo-Participle).*

Strong Verb

śḏm·kwy "I am hearing, or heard"

śḏm·ty "thou (mas. and fem.) art hearing, or heard"

&c. (See § 77.)

Duplicating Verb

ḳb·kwy "I am cool"

ḳb·ty "thou art cool"

&c.

1. The conditional stem or pseudo-participle is used:

a) In dependence upon another verb, like a participle, e.g. *w3ḥ·f wy wḏ3·kwy* "he laid me down when I was healed."

b) With the verb *ḫpr* "to become" in all its meanings, e.g. *tny ḫpr·w* "old age comes to pass."

2. See above § 79, 14.

§ 95. *The Causative Stem.*

Strong Verb

ś·śḏm·y "I cause to hear"

ś·śḏm·k "thou causest to hear"

&c.

Duplicating Verb

ś·ḳbb·y "I cause to be cool"

ś·ḳbb·k "thou causest to be cool"

&c.

1. Causatives are used more often with intransitive than with transitive verbs, e.g. *ś·nfr* "to make beautiful," *ś·ḫr* "to cause to fall."

2. Causatives of three consonants are treated like four-consonant verbs, and are quite regular, but two-consonant causatives take a feminine infinitive, e.g. *ś·mn·t* "to establish."

§ 96. *Other Stems.*

1. There are isolated forms which look like the Semitic Niphal, e.g. *n·ḏdḏd* "to endure" from *ḏd.*

2. There are also forms which repeat the final consonant, e.g. *śpdd* "to prepare"; and others which repeat two of the consonants, e.g. *śḫśḫ* "to hasten," *śd3d3* "to tremble."

§ 97. *Vocabulary.*

ḥʿy "to rejoice," *y3wy* "old age," *k3* "soul," "Ka," *h3y* "to advance," *wʿb* "to be clean," *ymy*(?) "make," "give," *r3-pr* "temple," *r3* "mouth," "entrance," *ytḥ* "to drag," *mnw* "monument," *ʿ3y* "to be great," *my* "like," "as," *ḏw* "mountain," *ymnty* "west," "right," *śmḥy* "east," "left," *r3-yt* "door," *bn·t* "harp," *mʿḥʿ·t* "tomb."

§ 98. *Exercises.*

CHAPTER XI

Weak Verbs

§ 99. *Weak Verb–Active–Indicative.*

Present Tense

śḏm·f

mry·y "I love"

mr·k "thou lovest"

&c.

śḏm·kꜣ·f

mr·kꜣ·y "thus I love"

mr·kꜣ·k "thus thou lovest"

&c.

Past Tense

śḏm·n·f

mr·n·y "I loved"

mr·n·k "thou lovedst"

&c.

śḏm·yn·f

mr·yn·y "then I loved"

mr·yn·k "then thou lovedst"

&c.

Future Tense

śḏm·ḫr·f

mr·ḫr·y "I shall love"

mr·ḫr·k "thou wilt love," or "love thou"

&c.

§ 100. *Weak Verb–Passive–Indicative.**

Present Tense

śḏm·tw·f

mr·tw·y "I am loved"

mr·tw·k "thou art loved"

&c.

Past Tense

śḏm·n·tw·f

mr·n·tw·y "I was loved"

mr·n·tw·k "thou wast loved"

&c.

§ 101. *Weak Verb–Emphatic.***

Present Tense

śḏm·f

mrr·y "I love"

mrr·k "thou lovest"

&c.

§ 102. *Imperative.*

mr "love thou" *mr·w* "love ye"

---

* The other parts of the *passive* can easily be constructed on the model of the forms in § 83.

** The other forms of the *emphatic* can easily be constructed on the model of the forms in §§ 84 ff.

§ 103. *Infinitive.*

mr·t	"to love"

§ 104. *Participles.*

mr	"having loved"
mrr·w	"loving"
mry	"loved"
mrr·w	"being loved"

§ 105. *Relatives.*

mrr·t·y	"that which I love"
mrr·t·k	"that which thou lovest"

&c.

§ 106. *Conditional Stem (Qualitative or Pseudo-Participle).*

mr·kwy	"I am loving, or loved"
mr·ty	"thou (mas. and fem.) art loving, or loved"
mr·w	"he is loving, or loved"
mr·ty	"she is loving, or loved"
mr·wyn	"we are loving, or loved"
mr·tywny	"ye (mas. and fem.) are loving, or loved"
mr·w	"they are loving, or loved"
mr·ty	"they (fem.) are loving, or loved"

§ 107. *Causative Stem.*

ś·mr·t "to cause to love"

§ 108. *Remarks on the Weak Verb.*

1. The weak consonant (*y* or *w*) is usually not written.

2. Weak verbs as well as causatives of two-consonant verbs take the feminine ending in the infinitive.

3. In weak verbs doubling often appears in the *śḏm·f*.

4. In the conditional or pseudo-participle, the final weak consonant (*y* or *w*) of the root is not written.

5. Passives of weak verbs usually omit the last weak consonant.

6. In the predicative the weak verbs do not have the last weak consonant *y* before the predicative ending *w*.

7. The plural ending *y* (later also *w*) of the imperative merges into the last weak consonant of weak verbs.

8. Weak verbs show the doubling in imperfect participles.

9. In relative forms, weak verbs double the last strong consonant.

§ 109. *Vocabulary.*

mśḏy "to hate," *drp* "to offer sacrifice," *šsp* "to take," *n-ʿ3·t-n* "because," *m-mʿ* "with," *y* "Oh!" *nṯr* "god," or *nṯry* "divine," *ḥtp* "offering," *ḫpy·t* "death," *ḳm3* "to create," *rnn* "to rear," "bring up," *ḥḳ3* "to rule over," *ḏ·t* "for ever," *mky* "to protect," *km·t* "Egypt," *ḫ3ś·t* "foreign country," *śr* "high official," or *św3y* "to pass by," *yny* "to bring," *ḥʿpy* "Nile."

§ 110. *Exercises.*

* Old form (*śwt*) of 3rd mas. sing. per. pronoun.

** Old form (*yr*) of the preposition *r*.

CHAPTER XII

Irregular Verbs

§ 111. *Irregular Verb–Active–Indicative.*

Present Tense

śḏm·f

dy·y "I give"

dy·k "thou givest"

&c.

śḏm·kꜣ·f

dy·kꜣ·y "thus I give"

dy·kꜣ·k "thus thou givest"

&c.

Past Tense

śḏm·n·f

rdy·n·y "I gave"

rdy·n·k "thou gavest"

&c.

śḏm·yn·f

rdy·yn·y "then I gave"

rdy·yn·k "then thou gavest"

&c.

Future Tense

śḏm·ẖr·f

rdy·ẖr·y "I shall give"

rdy·ẖr·k "thou wilt give," or "give thou"

§ 112. *Irregular Verb–Passive–Indicative.**

Present Tense

śḏm·tw·f

dy·tw·y "I am given"

dy·tw·k "thou art given"

&c.

Past Tense

śḏm·n·tw·f

dy·n·tw·y "I was given"

dy·n·tw·k "thou wast given"

&c.

§ 113. *Irregular Verb–Emphatic.***

Present Tense

śḏm·f

dydy·y "I give"

dydy·k "thou givest"

&c.

---

* The other parts of the *passive* can easily be constructed on the model of the forms in § 83.

** The other forms of the *emphatic* can easily be constructed on the model of the forms in §§ 84 ff.

§ 114. *Imperative.*

ymy	"give thou"
ymy·w	"give ye"

§ 115. *Infinitive.*

rdy·t	"to give"

§ 116. *Participles.*

rdy	"having given"
dydy	"giving"
rdy	"given"
dydy·w	"being given"

§ 117. *Relatives.*

dydy·t·y	"that which I give"
dydy·t·k	"that which thou givest"

&c.

§ 118. *Conditional Stem (Qualitative or Pseudo-Participle).*

dy·kwy	"I am giving, or given"
dy·ty	"thou (mas. and fem.) art giving, or given"
dy·w	"he is giving, or given"
dy·ty	"she is giving, or given"
dy·wyn	"we are giving, or given"
dy·tywny	"ye (mas. and fem.) are giving, or given"
dy·ty	"they are giving, or given"

§ 119. *Causative Stem.*

ś·rdy "to cause to give"

§ 120. *Vocabulary.*

wḏꜣ "to be glad," *wḏ* "to command," *gb* (*gbb*) the god Geb, *ḫtf* "according as," *nḫn* "to be young," *bw ẖr* "place at which," *wꜣ·t* "way," *m ḫd* "northward," *śnḏ* "fear," *ḥ·t* "fortress," "castle," *św* "the sun," "light," *hꜣy* "go away," "pour in," or , *yr, r*, used for emphasis "namely." It takes the pronominal suffixes. *šmśy* "to follow," *mˁ* "because," *mꜣˁ·t* "truth," *nb* "lord," *ḥtp dy nswt* "an offering which the king gives," *pr·t-r-ḫrw* "funeral offering."

§ 121. *Exercises.*

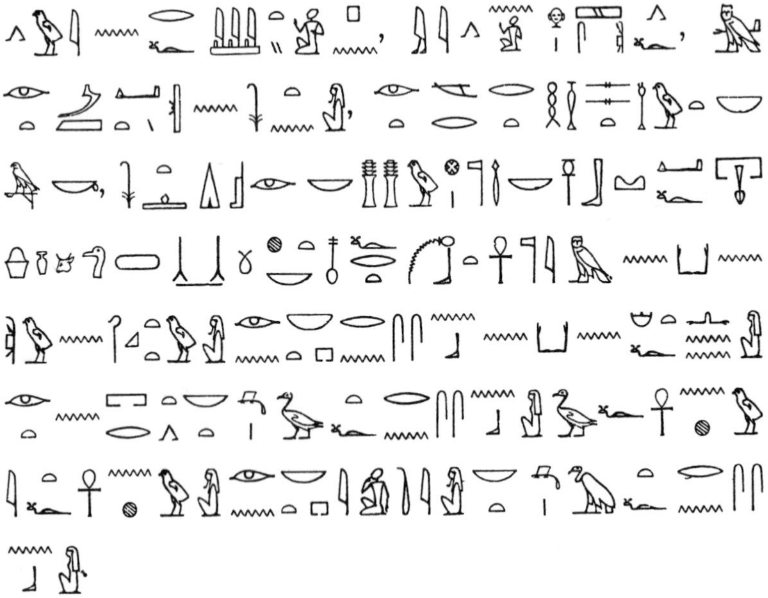

CHAPTER XIII

Auxiliary Verbs

§ 122. *The Auxiliaries* *yw* and * *wn* *wn·t* "to be."

1. With strong verbs:

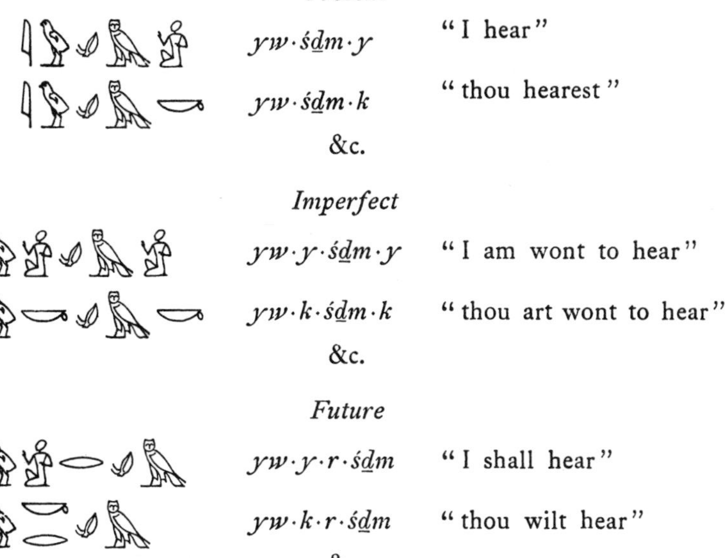

Present

yw·śdm·y	"I hear"
yw·śdm·k	"thou hearest"

&c.

Imperfect

yw·y·śdm·y	"I am wont to hear"
yw·k·śdm·k	"thou art wont to hear"

&c.

Future

yw·y·r·śdm	"I shall hear"
yw·k·r·śdm	"thou wilt hear"

&c.

2. With duplicating verbs:

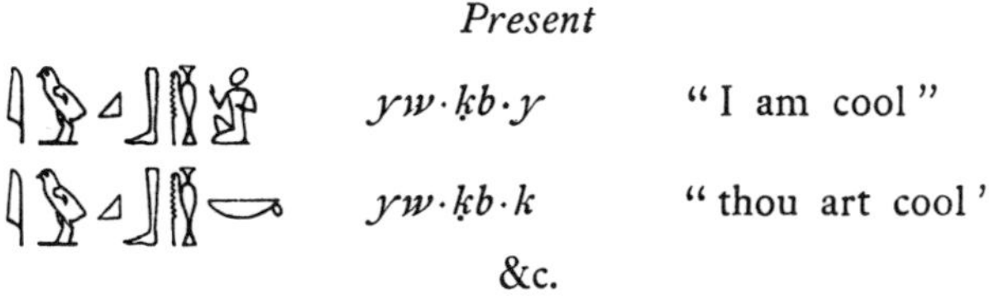

Present

yw·ḳb·y	"I am cool"
yw·ḳb·k	"thou art cool"

&c.

* The auxiliary *wn* is used in the same way as .

Imperfect

yw·y·ḳbb·y "I am wont to be cool"

yw·k·ḳbb·k "thou art wont to be cool"

&c.

Future

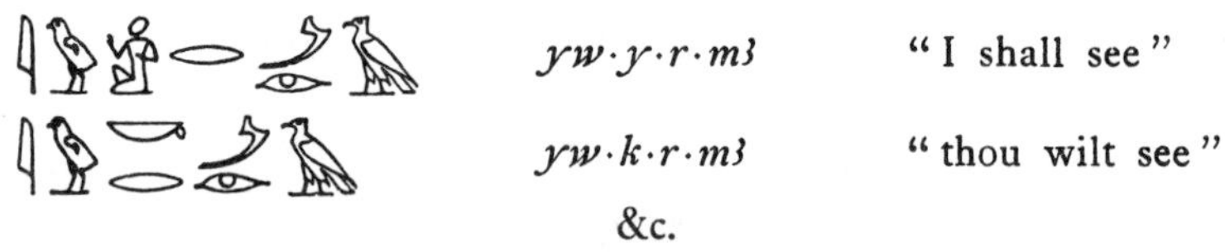

yw·y·r·m3 "I shall see"

yw·k·r·m3 "thou wilt see"

&c.

3. With weak verbs:

Present

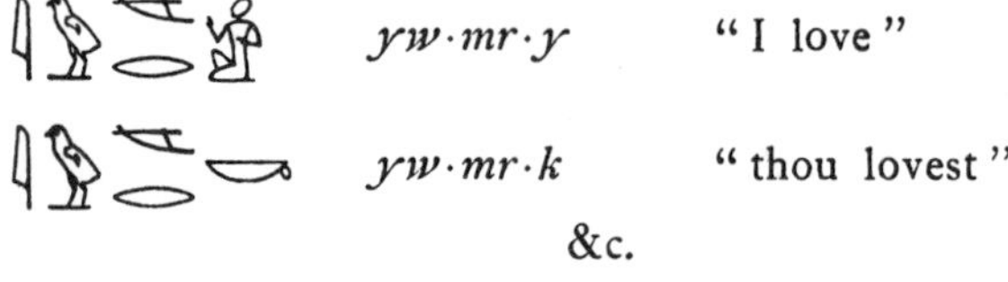

yw·mr·y "I love"

yw·mr·k "thou lovest"

&c.

Imperfect

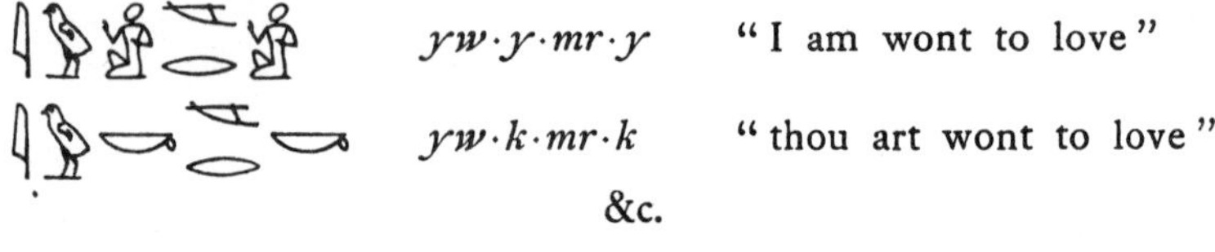

yw·y·mr·y "I am wont to love"

yw·k·mr·k "thou art wont to love"

&c.

Future

yw·y·r·mr·t "I shall love"

yw·k·r·mr·t "thou wilt love"

&c.

4. With irregular verbs:

Present

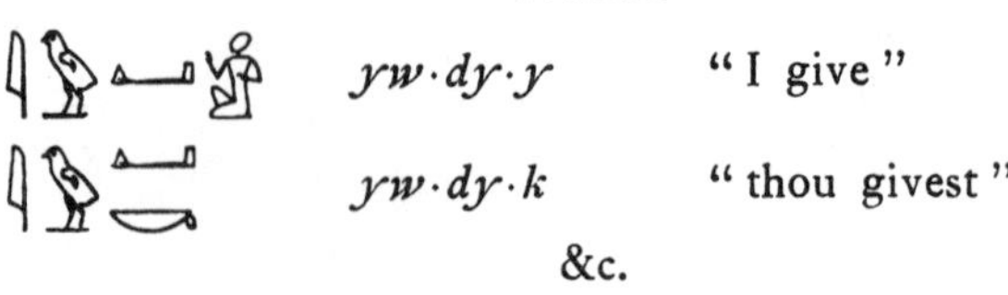

yw·dy·y "I give"

yw·dy·k "thou givest"

&c.

Imperfect

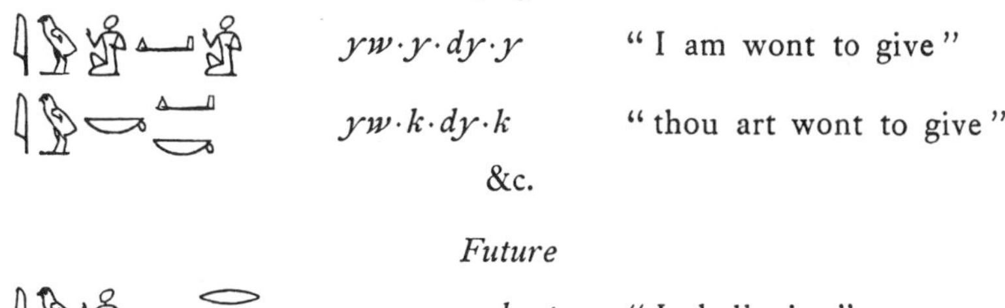

	yw·y·dy·y	"I am wont to give"
	yw·k·dy·k	"thou art wont to give"

&c.

Future

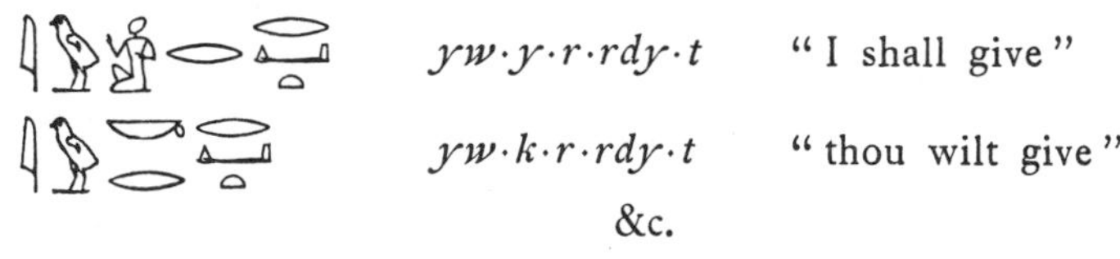

	yw·y·r·rdy·t	"I shall give"
	yw·k·r·rdy·t	"thou wilt give"

&c.

5. Remarks and examples:

a) These auxiliaries emphasize the idea in the verb, e.g. *yw ṯꜣ mdw* "the chicken chirps."

b) They are used also in nominal sentences, e.g. *yw ʿb·wy·ś m ḏꜣḏꜣ·k* "her horns are on thy head."

c) They are used with *ḥr* and the infinitive, e.g. *yw bw-nb ḥr dwꜣ nfrw·f* "everyone praised his beauty."

d) They are used in nominal sentences with the conditional (pseudo-participle), e.g. *yw·f śḏm·w* "he is hearing"; also with *ḥr* and the infinitive, e.g. *yw·f ḥr śḏm* "he is hearing."

e) The *r* of the future tense is also used in verbal sentences with or without the auxiliary, e.g. *yb n ḥm·k r·ḳbb* "the heart of thy majesty will be cool."

§ 123. The auxiliary *ʿḥʿ* "to stand" precedes the verb. It is usually rendered by "then." Transitive verbs follow this auxiliary in the *śḏm·f* form; intransitives take the conditional (pseudo-participle), e.g. *ʿḥʿ·n ṯḥn·n ḥm·f ḥnʿ·śn* "then his majesty came into conflict with them," [hieroglyphs] *ʿḥʿ·n rdy·kwy r yw* "then was I thrown on the island."

§ 124. The auxiliaries [hieroglyphs] *yyn*, [hieroglyphs] *prn*, and [hieroglyphs] *yw* are used in the same way as *ʿḥʿ*.

§ 125. The auxiliary [hieroglyph] *yry* "to do" is used with a following infinitive, e.g. [hieroglyphs] *yry·y šm·t* "I went" ("I did the going"). The past tense, *yry·n·f*, with [hieroglyphs] *pw* and an infinitive, is used in historical narrative, e.g. [hieroglyphs] *šm·t pw yry·n·f* "he went" ("to go was that which he did").

§ 126. The auxiliary [hieroglyphs] *pꜣ* "to have been," "to have had," especially in negative sentences, is used with the infinitive to denote a past condition or action, e.g. [hieroglyphs] *n sp pꜣ·tw yr·t myty·t* "never was done the like."

§ 127. *Vocabulary.*

[hieroglyphs] *drp* "to make libation," [hieroglyphs] *hꜣb* "to send out," "to go down," [hieroglyphs] *ʿḳ* "to enter," [hieroglyphs] *dp·t* "ship," [hieroglyphs] *yny* "to bring," [hieroglyphs] *ynw* "gifts," "offerings," [hieroglyphs] *pry* "to go out," [hieroglyphs] *nḏm* "to be sweet, well," [hieroglyphs] *ʿ* "side," "place," [hieroglyphs] *wꜣḥ* "put," "place," [hieroglyphs] *d·t* (?), *ḏr·t* "hand," [hieroglyphs] *mḥ* "to fill," "to be full," [hieroglyphs] *ś·ḫpr* "to cause to exist," [hieroglyphs] *šm* "to go," [hieroglyphs] *tw* "one."

§ 128. *Exercises.*

[hieroglyphs], [hieroglyphs]?

[hieroglyphs], [hieroglyphs], [hieroglyphs]

* Note this form *wn·yn·f śḏm·f.*

** Note the form *ḫr·f śḏm·f.*

CHAPTER XIV

Adverbs, Prepositions, and Conjunctions

§ 129. *Adverbs.*

There being no special adverbial form, adverbs are expressed in the following manner:

1. By an adjective, occasionally with the ending *w* or *t*, e.g. *wr·t* "very," "quite," *nfr·w* "well," *ḏ·t* "eternally"; *ꜣw yb·k my Rʿ ḏ·t* "thy heart is glad like Reʿ eternally."

2. By an adjective preceded by the preposition , e.g. *r mnḫ* "excellently," *r yḫ·t nb·t* "above all," *r ʿꜣ·t* "very."

3. By means of prepositional forms, e.g. *ym* "there," "yonder," "therein," "thereof," &c., *ḫnt*, *m-bꜣḥ*, *ḥr-ḥꜣ·t* "before," *ḫft* "in front," *ḏr-bꜣḥ* "formerly," *m-ḫt*, *m-śꜣ*, *ḥr-śꜣ*, *r-śꜣ*, *n-śꜣ* "afterward."

§ 130. *Prepositions.*

Prepositions may be divided into two classes, simple and compound. The following are examples of both classes; others will be found in the vocabulary. The following should be committed to memory.

1. *Simple prepositions:* When they are combined with suffixes they occasionally have a fuller writing, e.g. *ym·f* "in him," *yr·f* "to him."

m	"in," "at," "from," "with," "into," "out of," "among," "to," "of," "as," "like," "according to," "into," "by means of," &c.
r	"at," "by," "to," "into," "as far as," "toward," distributively of time, &c.
n	"for," "to," "because of," "in (of time)," "of," &c.
ḥr	"at," "in," "down," "upon," "with," "because of," "on account of," &c.
ẖr	"under"
ḫr	"with," "under" (during the reign of)
yn	used with the passive, and to emphasize the subject; also with the infinitive
mᶜ	"in possession of," "from," "by," "because of"
ḫft	"in front of," "according to," "corresponding to," "simultaneously with"
my	"like," "as"
ḥnᶜ	"together with"
ḫnt	"before," "at the head of"
tp	"upon"
ḏr	"when," "since"

2. *Compound prepositions:* They are generally simple prepositions combined with nouns. The following examples should be committed to memory.

m-bꜣḥ "before"

m-ḥꜣ·t "before," "at the head of"

m-ḥr	"in front of"
m-ḫt	"behind," "after"
m-dy	"together with"
n-mrw·t	"on account of," "in order that"
r-gś	"near," "at the side of"
ḥrw-r	"outside," "distant from"
r-śꜣ	"behind," "after"
ḥr-śꜣ	"behind," "after"
ḫft-ḥr	"in front of"
ẖr-ḥꜣ·t	"at the head of"

§ 131. *Conjunctions.*

Conjunctions may be divided into two classes, enclitics and absolute conjunctions.

1. *Enclitic conjunctions.*

yr, *yrf*, *rf*	"if," used for emphasis after the emphasized word
yś	"namely," "yes," "surely," introducing an explanatory addition
n-yś	"but not"
śwt, *ḥm*	"but," expressing the opposite to the preceding clause"
gr, *gr·t*	"but," "moreover," "also," "likewise"

2. *Absolute conjunctions.*

yśt, *śṯ* "since," "when," "behold," "however"

yśk "when"

ḫr "and," "but," "now," "since"

kꜣ used in directions, promises, threats, to strengthen what is stated

§ 132. *Vocabulary.*

wꜣśy "to be decayed," *hrw* "day," *mw* (*myw*) "water," *ḫʿy* "to shine," *śwꜣy* "to pass by," *šm* "to go," *wꜣḏ-wr* "sea," *mḥ* "ell," *ꜣw·t* "length," *yw* "island," *ḥfꜣw* "snake," *mry·t* "river-bank," *hꜣw* "near," *yꜣš*, *ʿš* "to call," *ḥknw* "praise," *nʿy* "to journey," "to sail," *ḫdy* "sail down stream," "northwards," *ẖnw* "residence."

§ 133. *Exercises.*

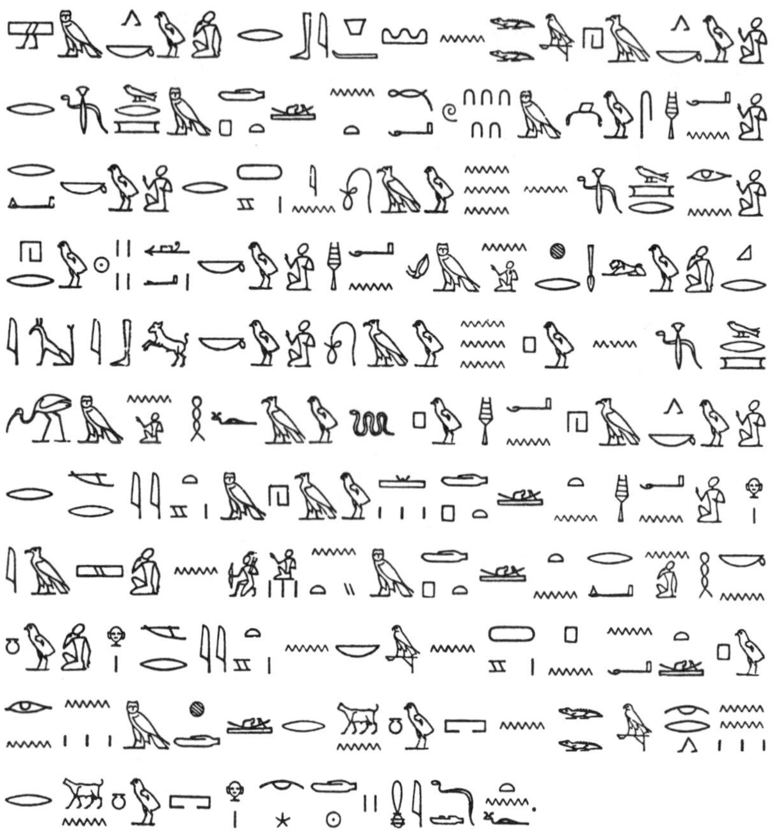

CHAPTER XV

Other Particles

§ 134. *Interjections.*

The two commonest interjections are *y* and *hꜣ* "O!", "Ha!", e.g. *y ʿnḫ·w* "O ye living!" They often stand before a proper noun which is then usually followed by *pn* "this," e.g. *hꜣ Ppy pn* "O thou king Pepi!"

The article *pꜣ* is often used in the nominative of address as an interjection, e.g. *pꜣ ytn ʿnḫ* "O thou living Aton!"

Certain interjections take a suffix, e.g. *ynḏ-ḥr·k wśyr nb ḥḥ* "Hail, thou, Osiris, lord of eternity!"

§ 135. *Particles of Negation.*

1. The negative *n* is used in nominal sentences, e.g. *n ntf pw mꜣʿ·t* "it is not he in truth"; in verbal sentences, e.g. *n rḫ·y św* "I know him not"; and with *sp* "time," e.g. *n sp* "never."

2. The negative *nn* is used in verbal sentences with a future meaning, e.g. *nn psš·f* "he will not divide"; with an infinitive, e.g. *wḏʿ nn rdy·t ḥr gś* "judging, not putting on one side"; and with a noun or pronoun, e.g. *nn mw ym nn wy ym* "no water is there, I am not there."

3. The emphatic negative is or *nfr n*, e.g. *nfr n yrtw mytt* "never was the like done."

4. The negative *ym* is used in optative and final sentences, e.g. *ym·k yr yḫ·t r·ś* "do not do anything against it."

5. The negative *tm* is used in conditional sentences, e.g. *tm-ḫr·ś ḫpr m ḥśb·t* "it does not become worms"; and in combination with *rdy*, meaning "to prevent," e.g. *kt nt tm rdy pr ḥf3w* "another (remedy) for preventing snakes from going forth."

6. The negative *m* is used in imperative and optative sentences, e.g. *m ʿ3 yb·k* "let not thy heart be proud."

7. The particle *nywty* is a negative relative, e.g. *nywty mw·t·f* "he who is without his mother."

8. Note the negative part of the phrase: *ntt nywtt* "that which is and that which is not."

§ 136. *The Relative Particle.*

The relative particle, *nty* "he who is," "that which is," is really a declinable pronoun (§ 69), and is used in relative clauses, e.g. *s nty mr* "a man who is ill."

§ 137. The particles *yr* and *my* (or *m*) are used in *Conditional* sentences, e.g. *yr gm·k d3yśw* "if thou findest a wise man"; *my dd·n·k* "if it is said to thee."

§ 138. *Interrogative Particles.*

1. The particle *mʿ* or *m* is very common, and occurs at the end of a sentence, e.g. *yrtw nn my mʿ* "like what is this done?"

2. At the beginning of a sentence [hieroglyphs] is used with [hieroglyphs] *yn*, e.g. [hieroglyphs] *yn mꜥ ḏd św* "who says it?"

3. The particle [hieroglyphs] *yn* or [hieroglyphs] *ynyw* is used in rhetorical questions, e.g. [hieroglyphs] *yn ꜥwꜣy·tw·y r·f m yꜣ·t·f* "shall I be robbed upon his place?"

4. The particle [hieroglyphs] *ptry* or [hieroglyphs] *pty* always stands at the beginning of a sentence, e.g. [hieroglyphs] *pty ꜣḥ·t·f* "what is his field?"

5. The particle [hieroglyphs] *trw* always follows the first word of the sentence, e.g. [hieroglyphs] *yn yw trw śḫꜣ·n·k* "didst thou remember?"

6. Other interrogative particles:

[hieroglyphs]	*yšśt*	"who?" "what?"
[hieroglyphs]	*ysy*	" "
[hieroglyphs]	*ysnw*	"when?"
[hieroglyphs]	*tn*	"where?"

§ 139. *Emphatic Particles.*

1. The particle [hieroglyphs], [hieroglyphs] *yr* "but," "now," "namely," "verily," generally begins a sentence, e.g. [hieroglyphs] *yr ntt nb·t m sš śḏm śt* "verily, all that is in writing, hear it."

2. The particle [hieroglyphs], [hieroglyphs] *yr·f* takes second place in a sentence, e.g. [hieroglyphs] *ḥḏ·n yr·f tꜣ* "when the earth became bright."

3. Both *yr* and *yr·f* are used for emphasis after the imperative, when they take a suffix, e.g. [hieroglyphs] *ꜥḥꜥ yr·k* "stand up, thou"; and also in interrogative sentences. (§ 154.)

4. The particle *yn* emphasizes the subject of a sentence, but it is not translated, e.g. *yn ḥm·f rdy yr·t·f* "his majesty caused that it be made."

§ 140. *Other Particles.*

1. The adverbial particle *wy* "how," "pray," follows the first word of a sentence, e.g. *nḏm wy ym3·t·k* "how beautiful is thy goodness."

2. The particle *mᶜ*, later *mᶜ·k* or *m·k* "behold," stands at the head of a sentence, and often immediately precedes the subject.

§ 141. *Vocabulary.*

pḥ "to reach," *ḏr* "since," *rk* "time," *pśš* "to divide," *y3·t* "place," "holy place," *3ḫw* "the blessed ones," *mr* "overseer," *śḳdy* "to sail," *yry-ᶜ·t* "officer," *k3·t* "work," *k3wty* "workman," *ḫr·t* "necropolis," "grave," *sš* "book," "writing," *mr* "canal," *śm3* "to kill," *ḫᶜy* "to shine," *wbn* "to rise (sun)."

§ 142. *Exercises.*

* Thutmose III.

SYNTAX

CHAPTER XVI

The Sentence in General

§ 143. *Verbal Sentences.*

For verbal sentences, see §§ 38–39.

§ 144. *Nominal Sentences.*

1. For a general description of nominal sentences, see §§ 37 and 40.

2. The usual order of words is: Subject, predicate, but for emphasis the order is reversed, e.g. *nfr mṯny* "good is my way."

3. Nominal sentences are used to express a simple act, e.g. *mʿk·wy m-bꜣḥ·k* "behold, I am before thee"; to express circumstance, e.g. "thou ascendest *wr·t m ḫt·k* when a greater one is behind thee"; and to express a relative idea, e.g. *s śt·t m nḥb·t·f* "a man on whose neck are swellings."

4. Nominal sentences often have *pw*, e.g. *pẖr·t pw* "it was medicine"; and sometimes *m*, e.g. *yb·y m śnw·y* "my heart was my companion."

5. Nominal sentences are introduced by *yw* "to be," e.g. *yw wꜣt·f wʿ·t ẖr mw* "its one side was under water"; and by *wnn* "to be," e.g. *wn yn nfr śt ḥr yb·śn* "it was good for their heart."

§ 145. *Order of Words in Sentences.*

1. Note what has been said about the order of words in §§ 38 and 144, 2.

2. Furthermore: *a*) When the subject and both objects are nouns, the order is, Subject–Accusative–Dative, e.g. *rdy·n nswt nb n b3k·f* "the king gave gold to his servant"; *b*) When the subject and objects are partly pronouns, the pronouns precede the nouns, e.g. "the king gave me gold," "the king gave it to his servant," "he gave me gold"; *c*) When both objects are pronouns, the suffix precedes the absolute pronoun, e.g. "the king gave it to me," "he gave it to me."

§ 146. *Emphasis.*

Emphasis is expressed in the following manner:

1. By irregular word-order, e.g. *t3·n pḥ·n św* "we have reached our land (our land, we have reached it)."

2. By means of the particle *yr*, e.g. *yr ntt nb·t m sš śdm śt* "all which is in a book, hear it."

3. By means of the particle *yn*, which emphasizes the subject, e.g. *yn ḥm·f rdy·f* "his majesty it was who gave."

4. By means of *r*, *yr*, with a suffix, after the emphasized word, e.g. *rdy·k r·k ny* "give thou to me." In later times an unchangeable *r·f*, *yr·f*, was used, e.g. *pr·t·y r·f* "when I went out."

§ 147. *Ellipse.*

1. Very often omitted words must be understood. This is usual in poetry. It is also common in comparisons, e.g. *ś·ȝw·f yb n bȝk·y ym my ḥḳȝ n ḫȝś·t nb·t* "he makes glad the heart of my servant even as (the heart of) the prince of any country."

2. Almost any part of a sentence may be omitted, when the context makes it clear what it should be, e.g. *yr·n·s m mnw·s* "she made (this) as her monument."

3. Other examples of ellipses are: The omission of *ḏd* "to say," e.g. *yn Rᶜ* "Reᶜ says"; *yn·śn* "they say"; *nṯrw ḥr* "the gods say."

§ 148. *Vocabulary.*

ymȝ·t "graciousness," *ḥs·t* "praise," *rwyy* "to flee," *hd* "hero," *wȝy* with "to be far from," *dw* "evil," *ᶜš* "to call," *. wr* "prince," *mnḫ* "to be pleasant," *ṯsw* "to command," *ḥśḳ* "to cut off," *yty* "king," *tyw* "yes," *ymy* (?) "give," "allow," *y* "Oh!", *rmṯ* "mankind," *mk* "behold," *yry* "belonging to," "of such a nature," *mn·t* "anything," *m-myt·t* "likewise."

§ 149. *Exercises.*

* The stroke \ is often written instead of a determinative.

CHAPTER XVII

Various Kinds of Sentences

§ 150. *Negative Sentences.*

1. Read again § 135.

2. Principal sentences are made negative by means of *n*, later *nn*. These particles always stand first in a sentence, e.g. *n rḫ·y św* "I know him not."

3. Dependent sentences are made negative by the auxiliary verbs *tm* and *ymy* "not to be," "not to have," e.g. *tm·f yry bw nfr* "he does nothing good"; N N *r3 n tm wnm N* "charm that N be not eaten."

4. Relative sentences are made negative by means of the particle *nyw·ty*, *nyw·tt* "who has not," "who is not." The particle agrees in gender and number with the noun, which it follows, e.g. *nyw·ty yh·t·f* "he who has not got his things." It can also be used as a substantive, e.g. "that which does not exist."

5. Commands are made negative by means of (later) *m*, e.g. *m yry* "do not."

§ 151. *Temporal Sentences.*

1. Dependent temporal sentences sometimes precede and sometimes follow the principal sentence, e.g. *ḥd·n t3 pḥ·n·y* "when the earth had become light, I arrived"; *d^c pr yw·n m w3d-wr* "a storm arose, (as) we were on the sea."

2. Dependent temporal sentences may or may not have a particle of dependence, e.g. *yw wp·n·f r3·f r·y yw·y ḥr h̲·t·y* "he opened his mouth against me (while) I was on my belly"; *ḫʿ·yn ḥm·f r śm3 m-ḫt śd̲m ś·t* "his majesty appeared to do battle, after he had heard it."

§ 152. *Conditional Sentences.*

1. Most conditional sentences have no conditional particle, e.g. *ḥtp·k m y3ḫ·t ymn·tt t3 m kwkw* "when thou settest in the western horizon, the earth is in darkness."

2. The conditional particle is *yr* "if," e.g. *yr gm·k d̲3yśw ḫ3m ʿwy·k* "if thou findest a wise man, bend thy arm (salute)."

§ 153. *Final Sentences.*

1. Final sentences as a rule have no introductory particle, e.g. *d̲d·n·f ʿḥ3·f ḥnʿ·y ḫmt·n·f ḥwt·f wy* "he said, 'he would fight with me; he thought, he would smite me."

2. Final sentences often follow *rdy* "to cause," "to make" *rdy·t m3·śn św* "to make them see the sun."

§ 154. *Interrogative Sentences.*

1. Read again § 138.

2. Interrogative sentences are usually introduced by a particle (§ 138), often followed by the enclitic , *yr·f (r·f)*, e.g. *yn mʿ yr·f yn·f św* "who brings it?"

§ 155. *Relative Sentences.*

1. Read again *Relative Pronouns* (§ 69), *Relatives* (Verbal §§ 75 and 90), *The Relative Particle* (§ 136).

2. Relative sentences may be introduced without any particle, and may have no external sign of relationship, e.g. *pꜣ tꜣ-ḥḏ ddw·ṯn n·y* "the white bread which thou givest to me."

3. Other relative sentences have a verb in the relative form (§ 90), e.g. *ḫꜣś·t nb·t rw·t·n·y r·ś* "each country to which I went."

4. Many relative sentences are introduced by relative pronouns (§ 69), e.g. *pꜣ tꜣ nty rdy·n·y n·ṯn św* "the bread which I have given to you."

5. Relative pronouns are used as nouns in relative sentences, e.g. *nty·t nb·t ym·f* "all which is in it."

6. For the negative of relative sentences, see § 150, 4.

§ 156. *Vocabulary.*

tp-ꜥ "before," *śꜣḥ* "to reach," *śpr* "to arrive," "to come," *wꜣḥ* "to last," "to be happy," *śwḏ* "to convince," *ẖrd* "child," *my* "when," *ḥsy* "to praise," *n·t* "city," *šdy* "to read," *ḫrp* "stela," "tombstone," *r-ḏd* introduces a final clause, *r-nty·t* introduces a final clause, *wꜣy* "to be inclined to," *bšṯ* "to revolt," *ꜥḥꜣ* "to fight," *yry* "belonging to," *rd* "foot," *sp* "time," indicates that what precedes is to be read twice, *ḫnd* "to tread," *pry* "a hero," *mꜣꜥ·t* "truth," *bw* in *bw nb* "all men."

§ 157. *Exercises.*

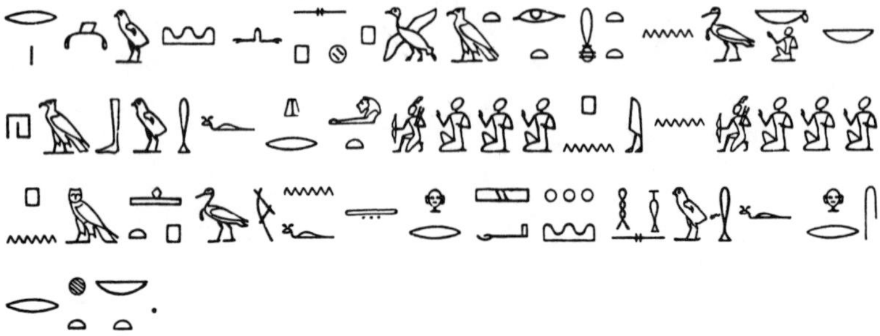

CHRESTOMATHY

I

Some Short Pieces from Various Sources

1. *Admiral Ahmose relates his deeds*

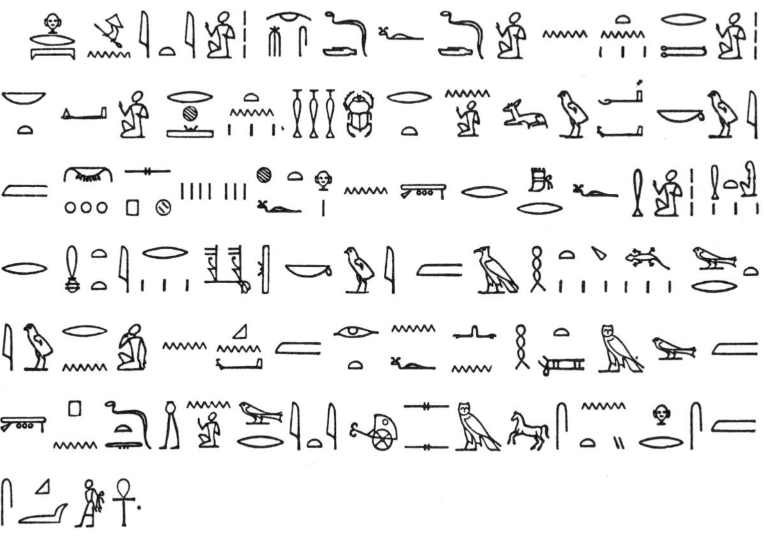

2. *Death of Thutmose III and accession of Amenophis II*

3. *Dedication of a Temple by Thutmose III*

4. *Victory of Thutmose III over Naharina*

5. *An address to Thutmose III*

6. *Amenemheb relates his warlike deeds*

7. *Nubian war under Thutmose II*

8. *Marriage Scarab of Amenophis III*

9. *Battle of Kadesh under Rameses II*

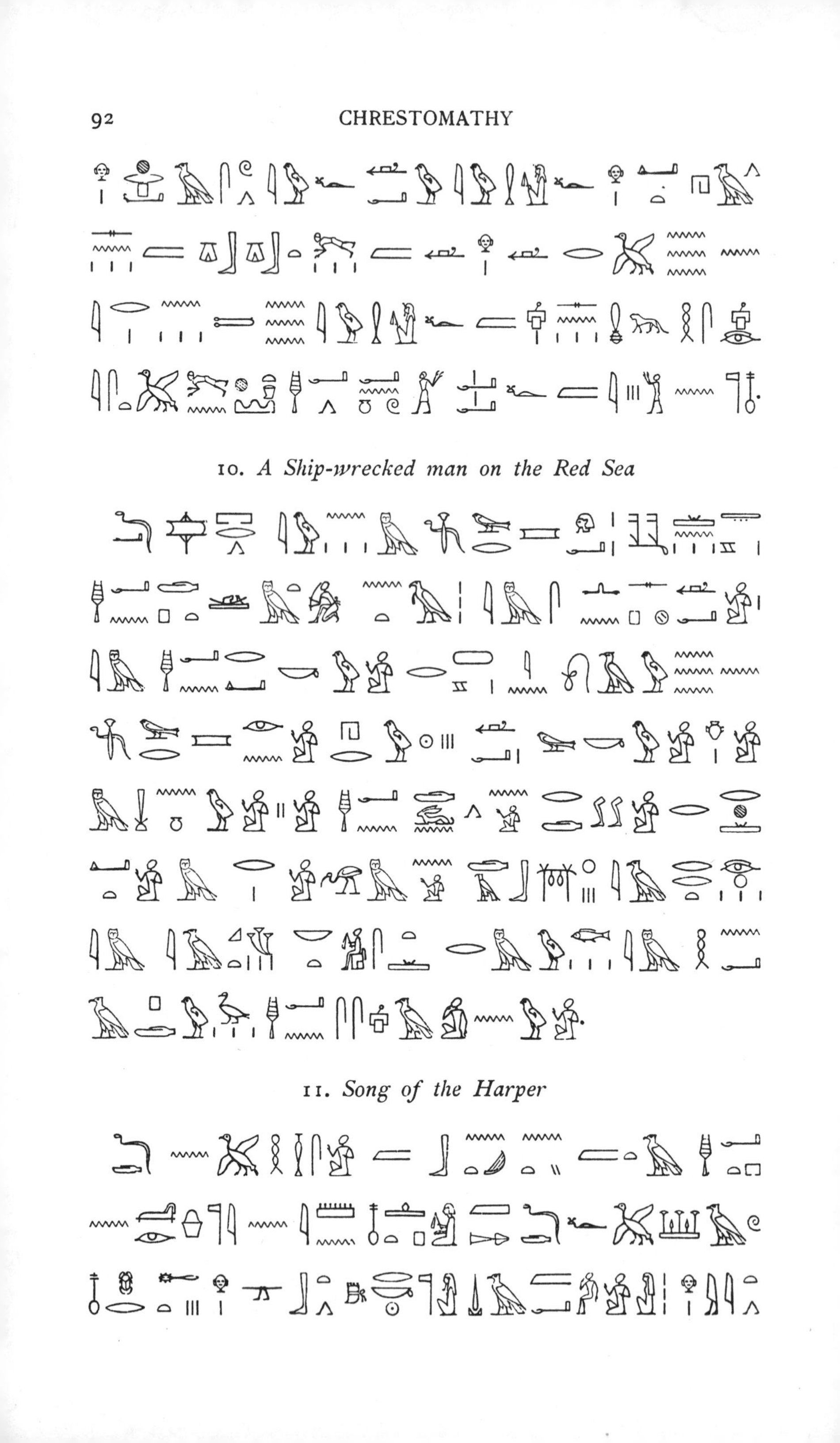

10. *A Ship-wrecked man on the Red Sea*

11. *Song of the Harper*

12. *A Dragon-god's Prophecy*

13. *Horus appointed World-ruler*

14. *A Hymn to Osiris*

15. *A Prayer for the Dead*

16. *Examples of Offering-formulae*

a)

b)

c)

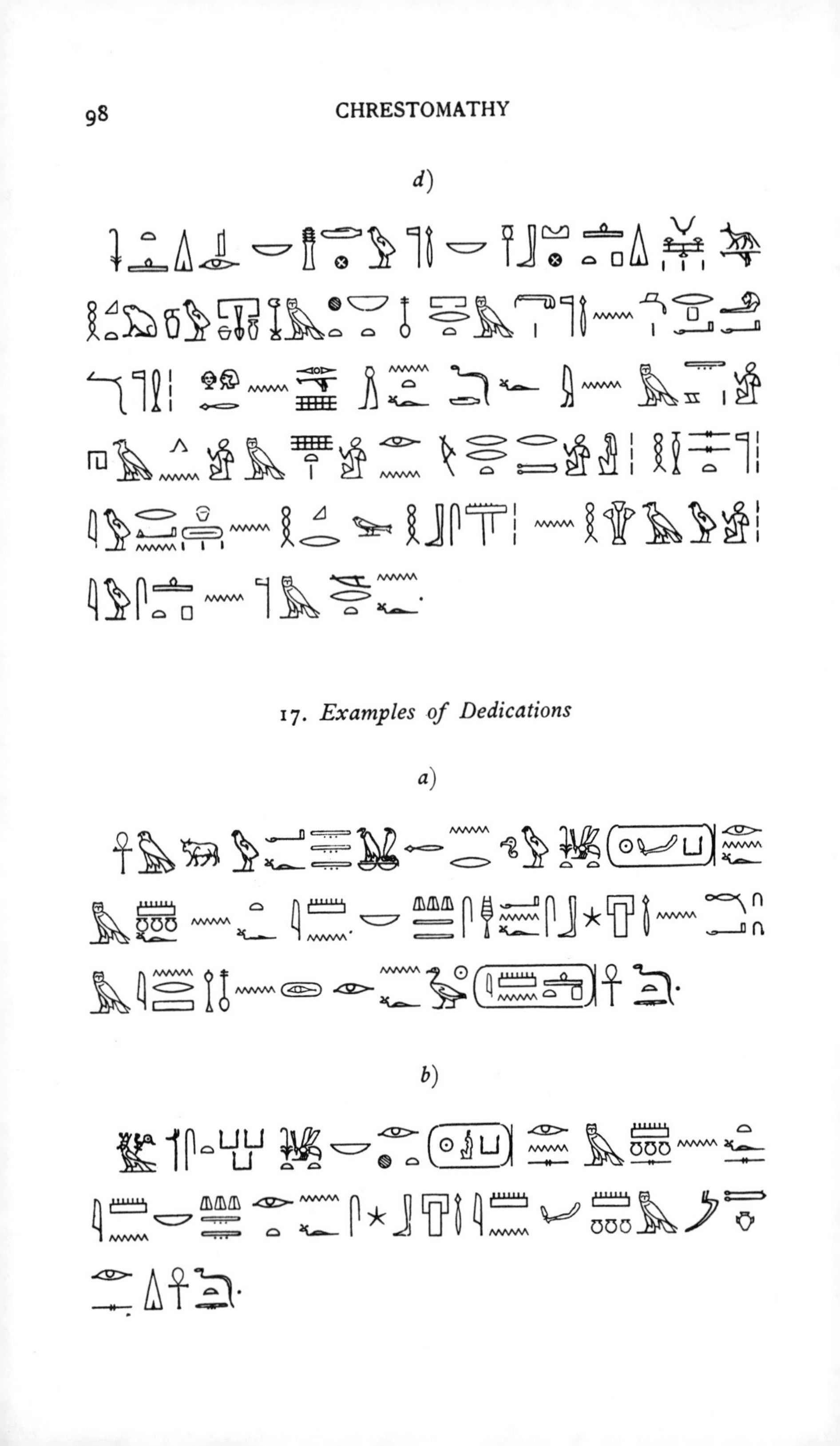

d)

17. *Examples of Dedications*

a)

b)

c)

d)

II

Extracts from the Pyramid Texts

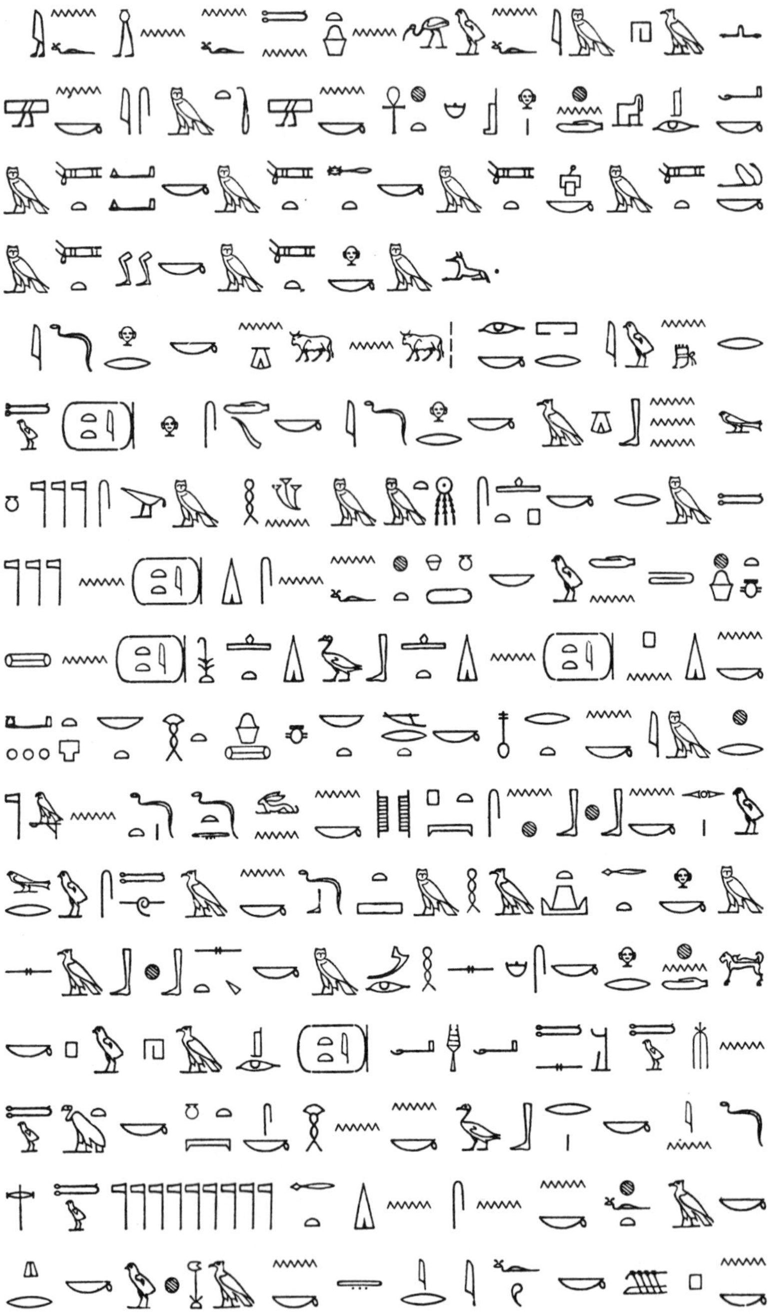

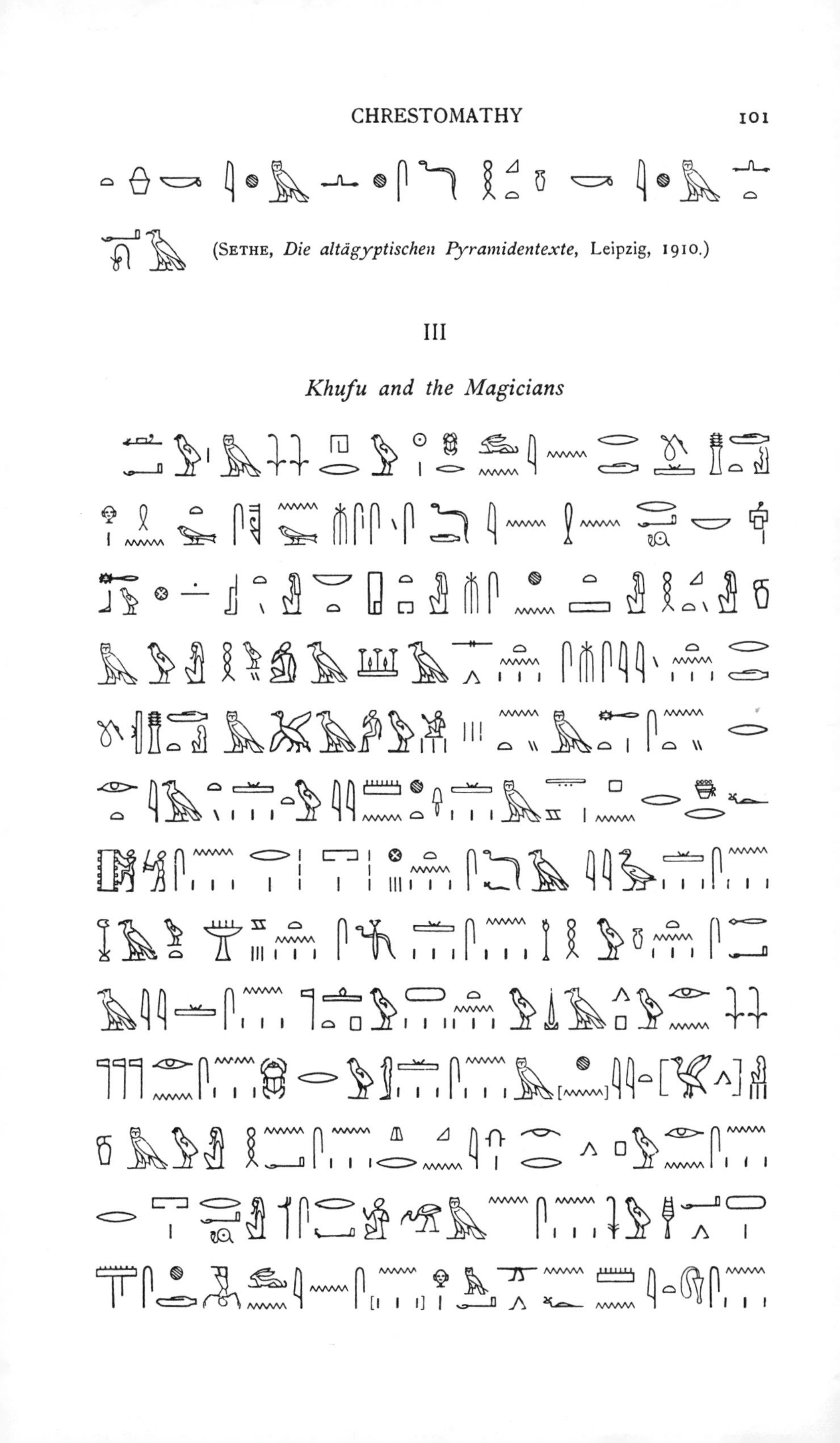

(SETHE, *Die altägyptischen Pyramidentexte*, Leipzig, 1910.)

III

Khufu and the Magicians

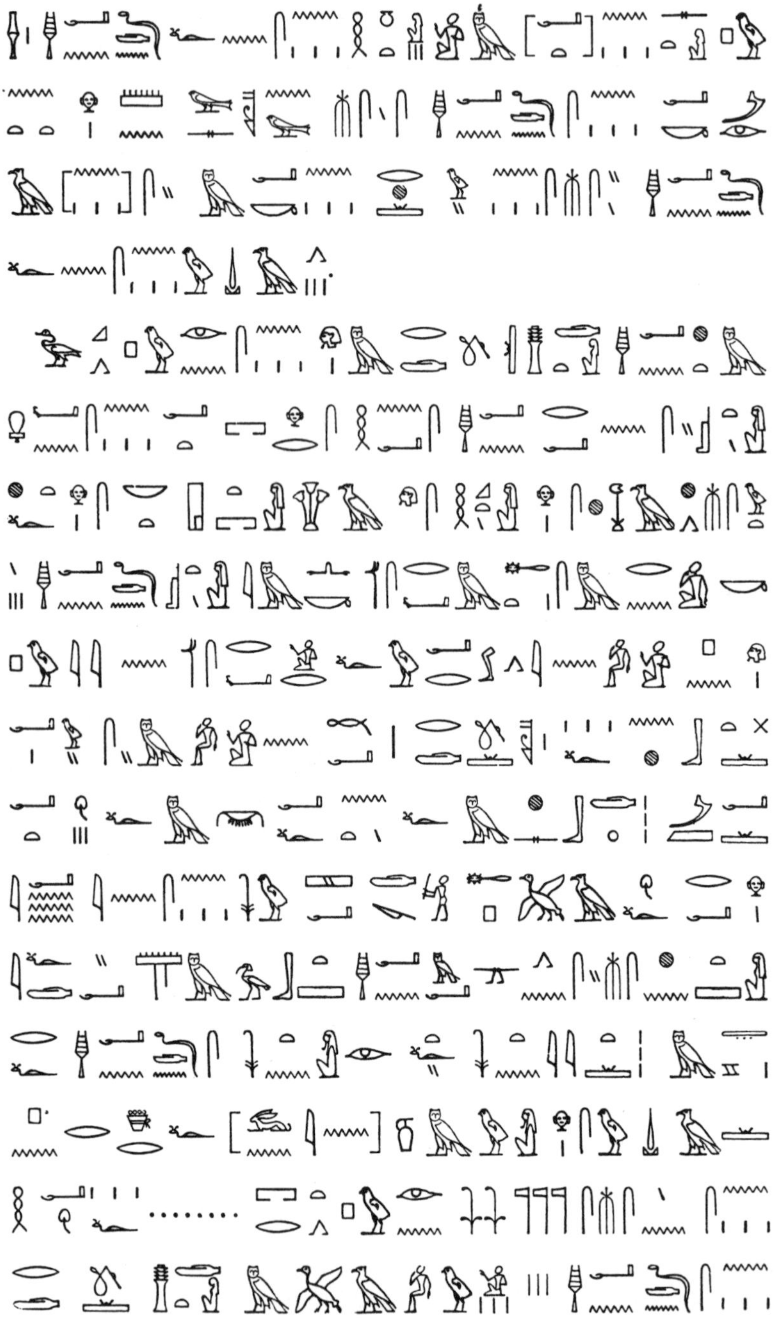

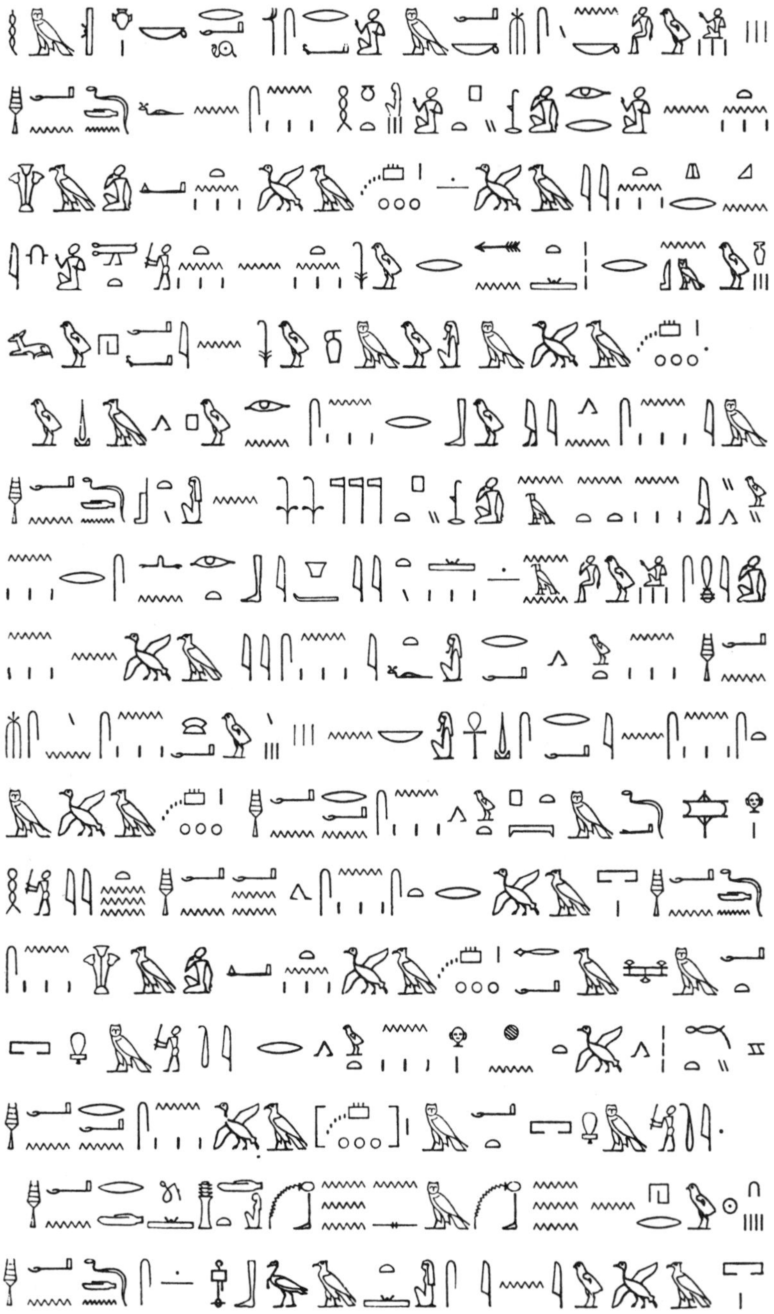

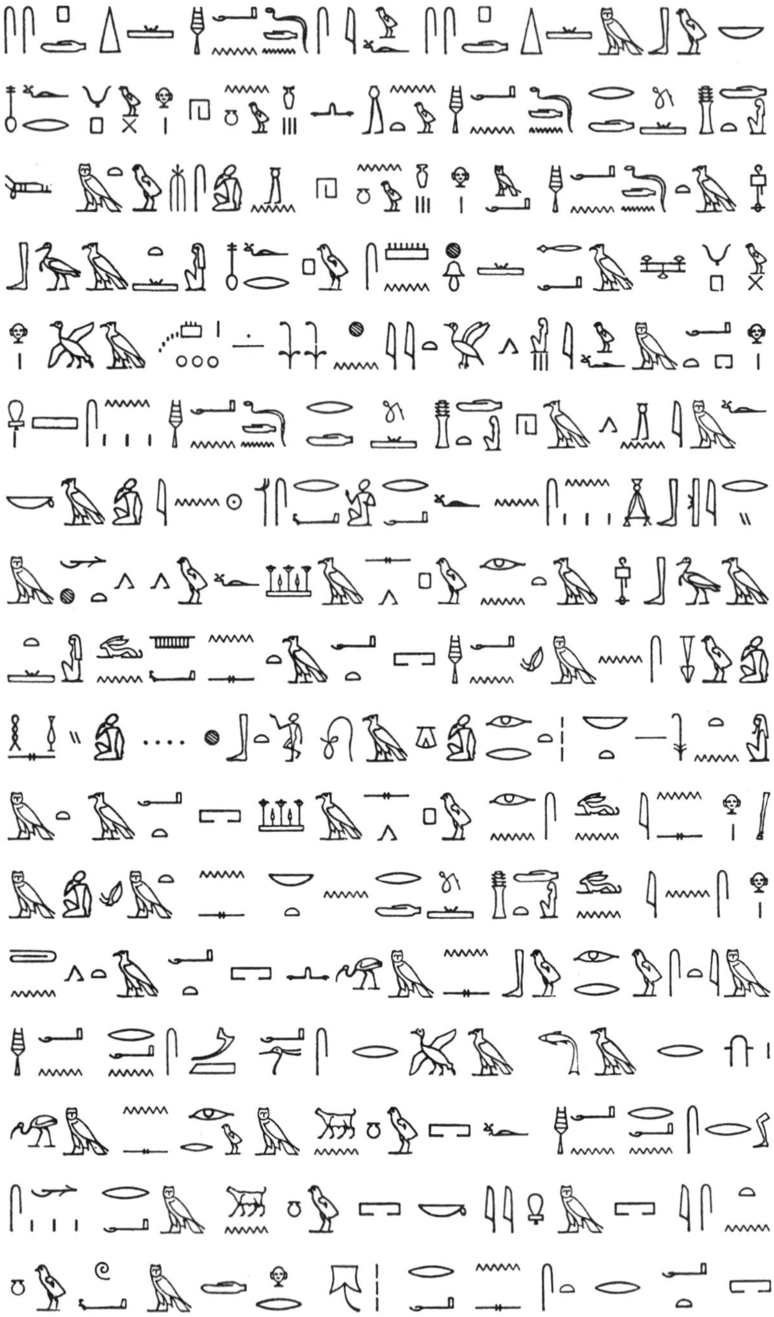

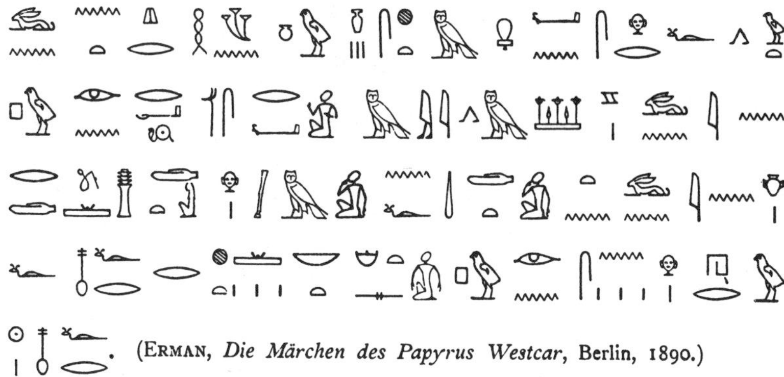

(Erman, *Die Märchen des Papyrus Westcar*, Berlin, 1890.)

IV

From the Precepts of Ptaḥ-Ḥotep

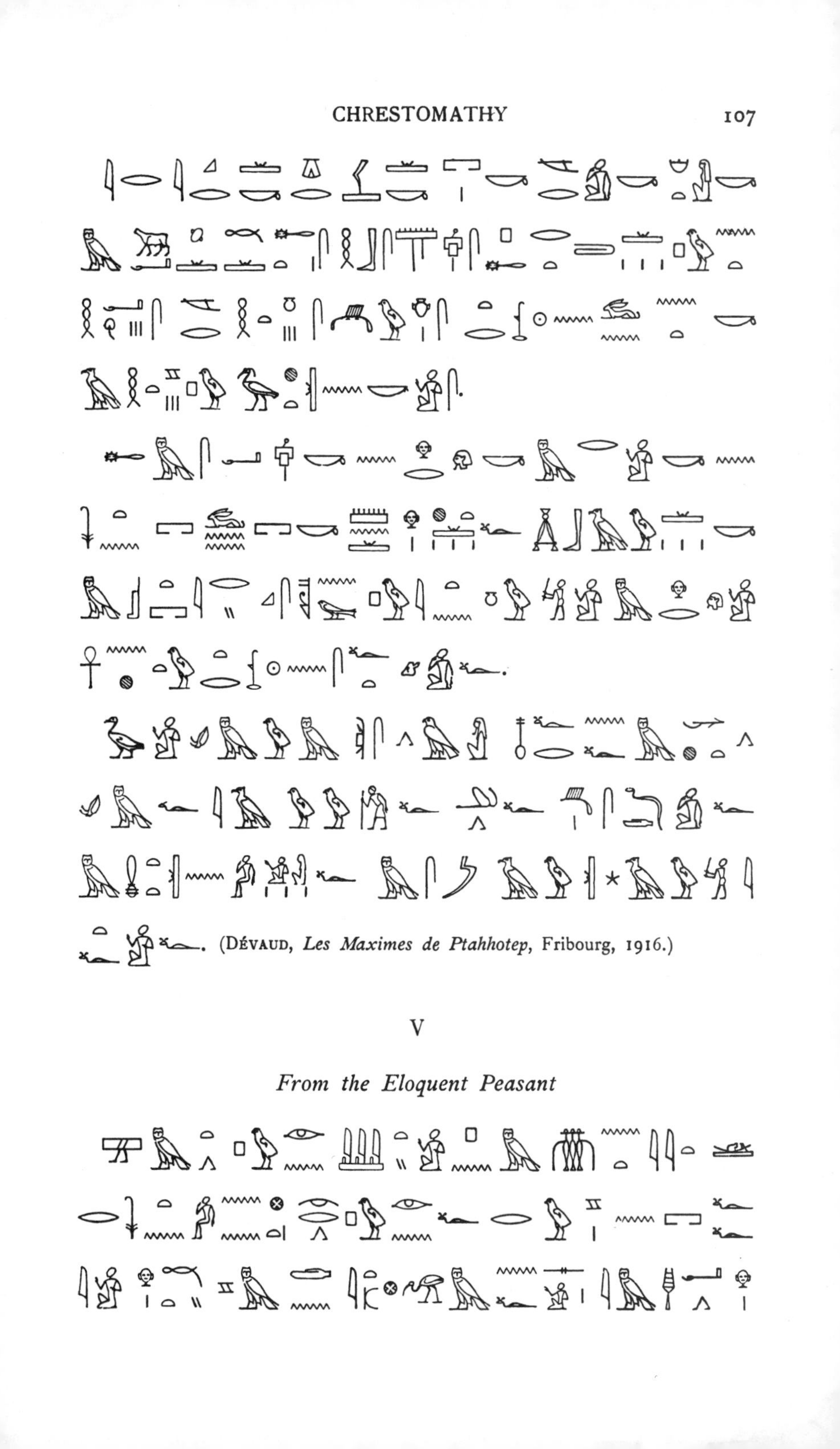

(DÉVAUD, *Les Maximes de Ptahhotep*, Fribourg, 1916.)

V

From the Eloquent Peasant

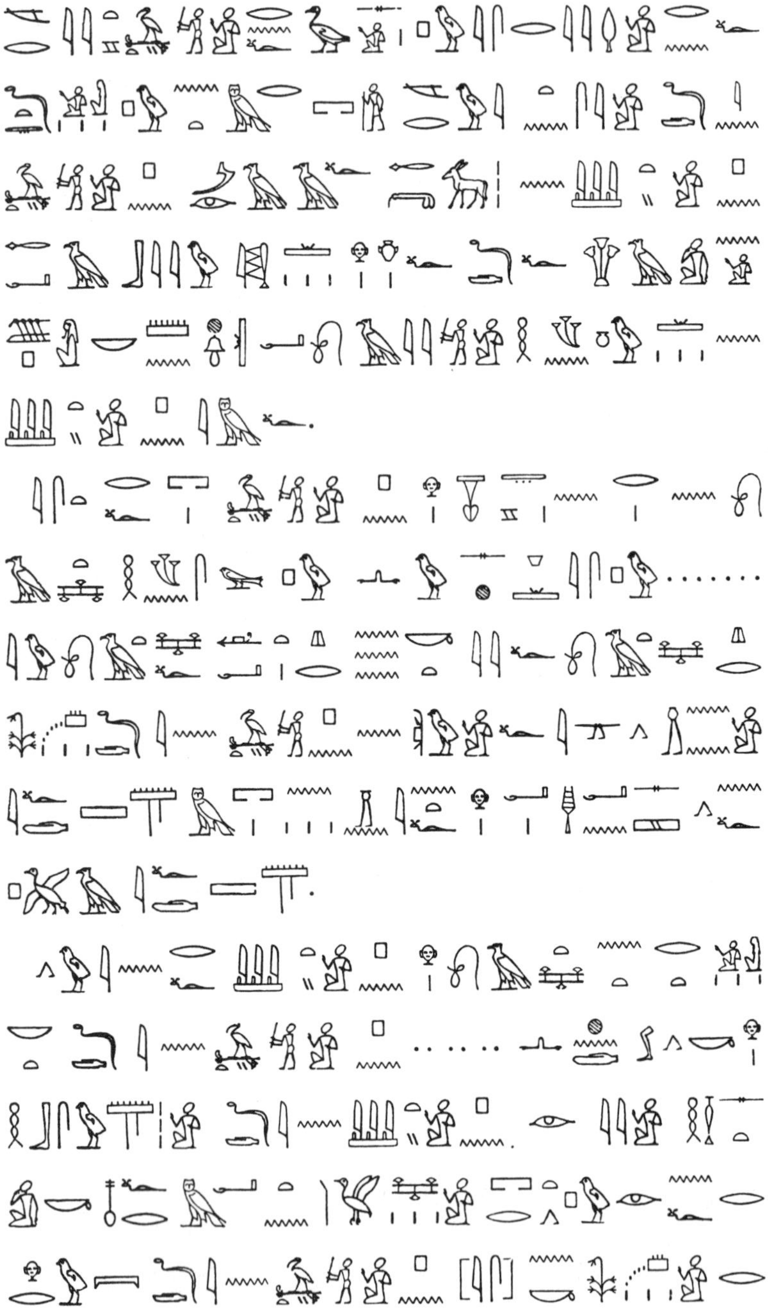

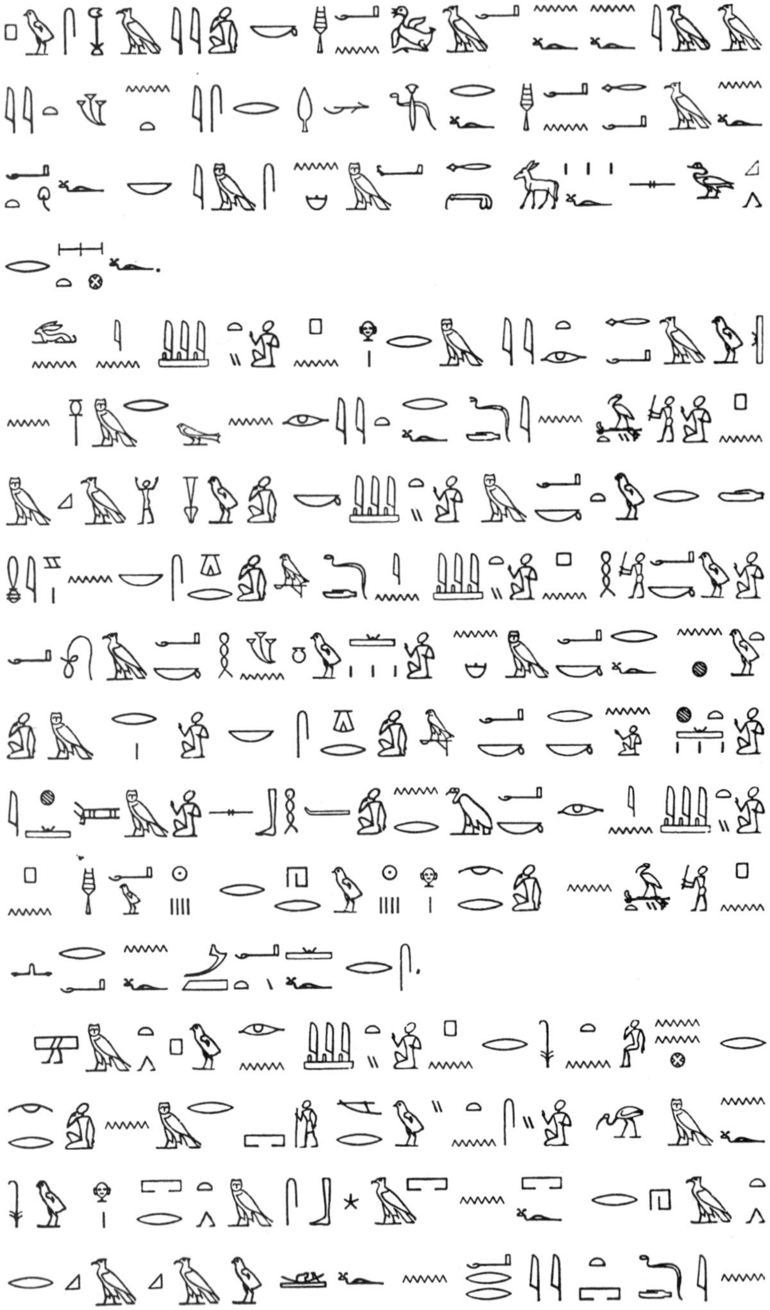

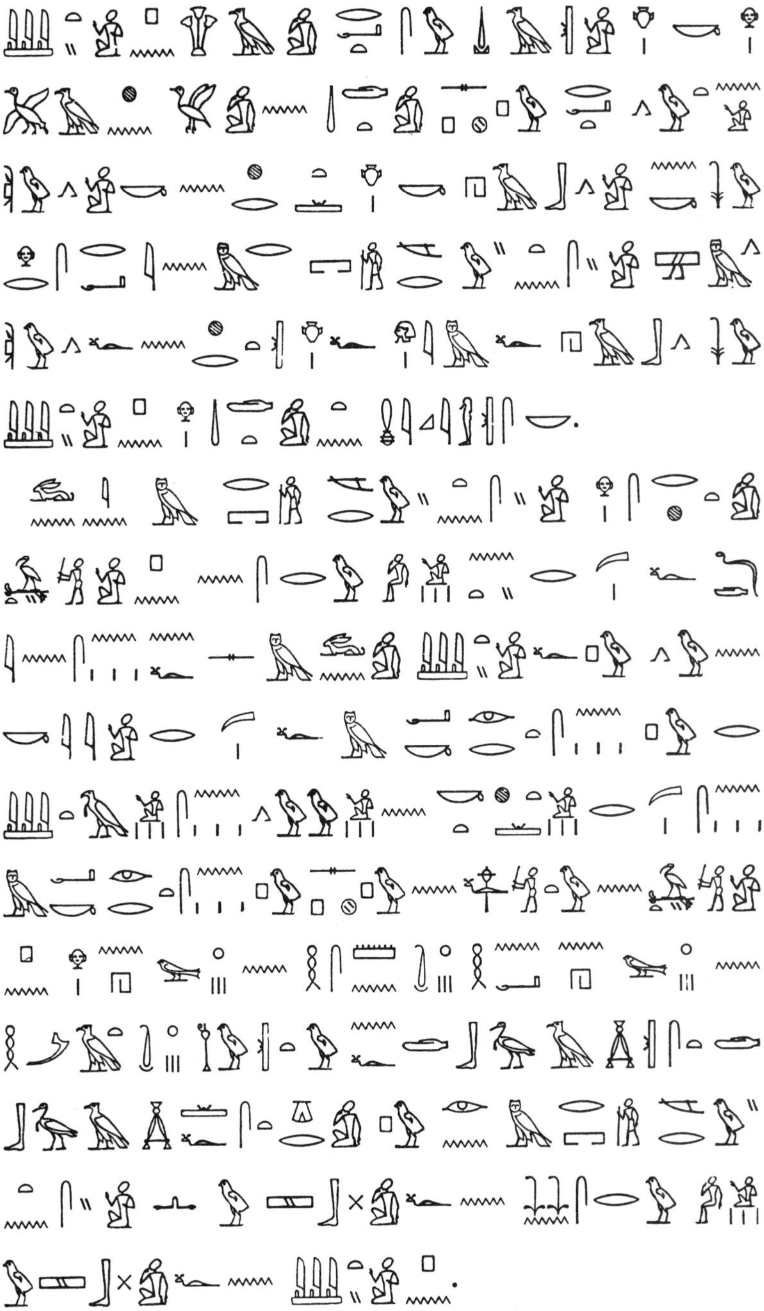

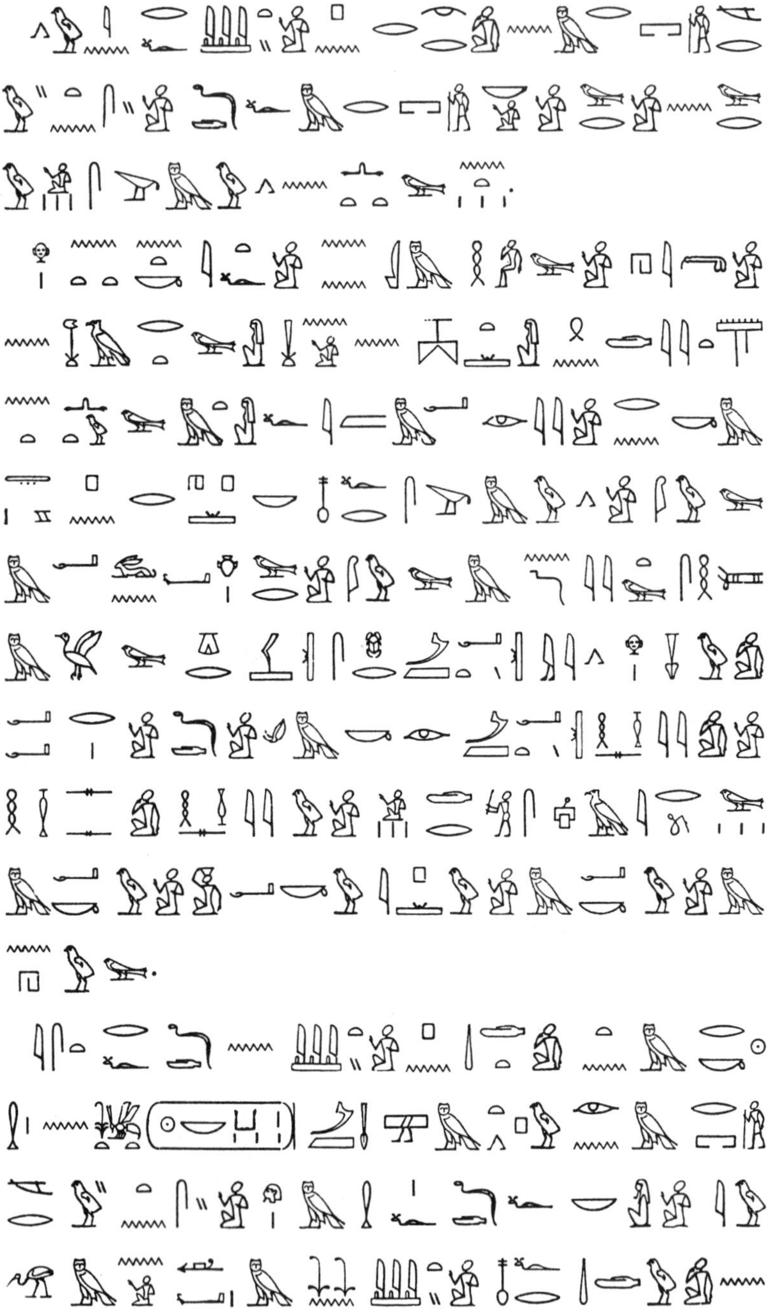

(VOGELSANG-GARDINER, *Die Klagen des Bauern*, Leipzig, 1908.)

VI

From the Memoirs of Sinuhe

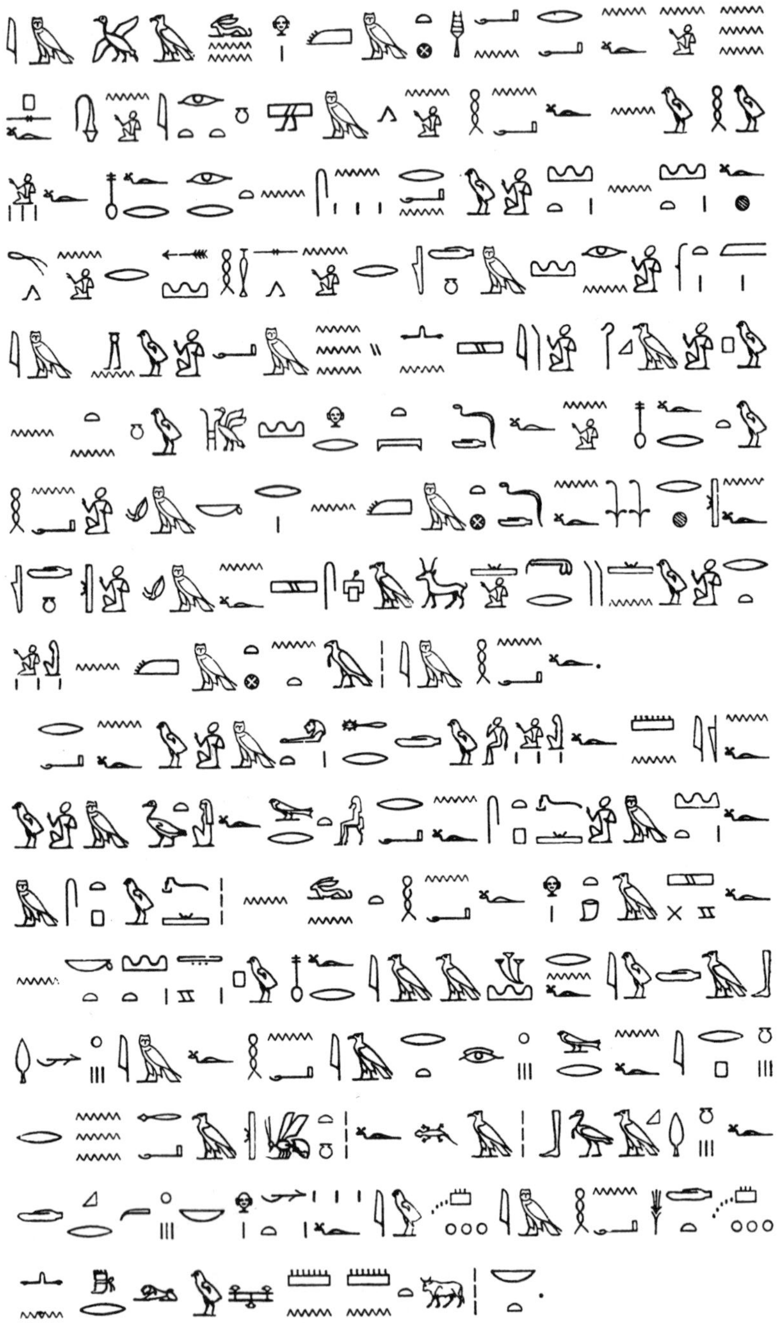

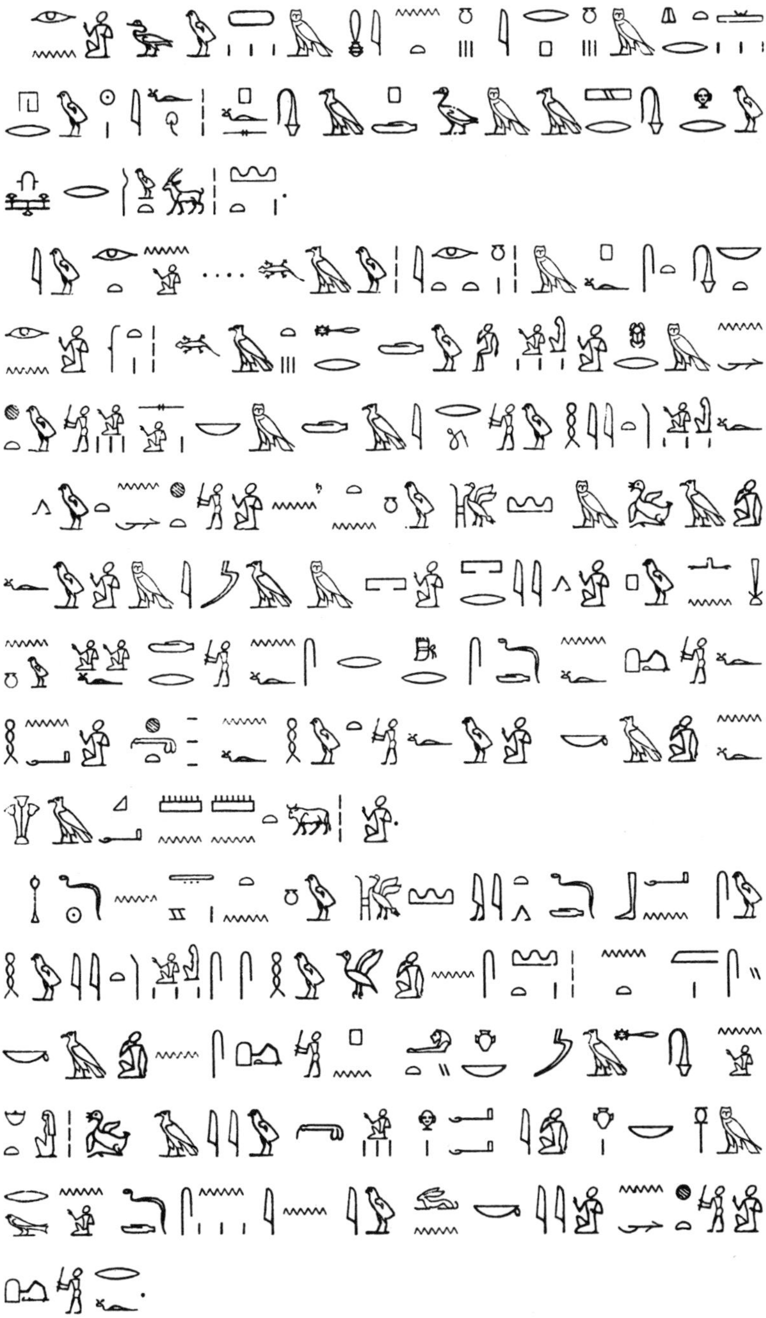

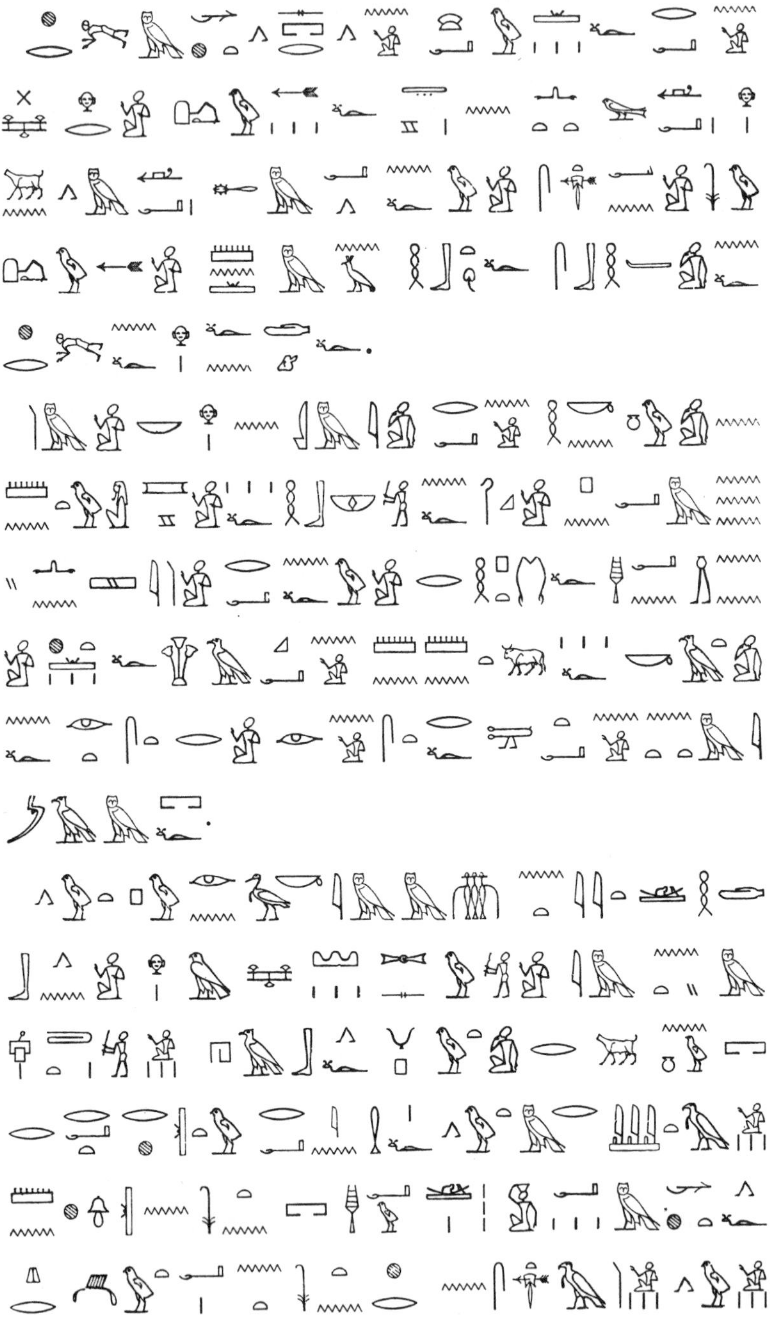

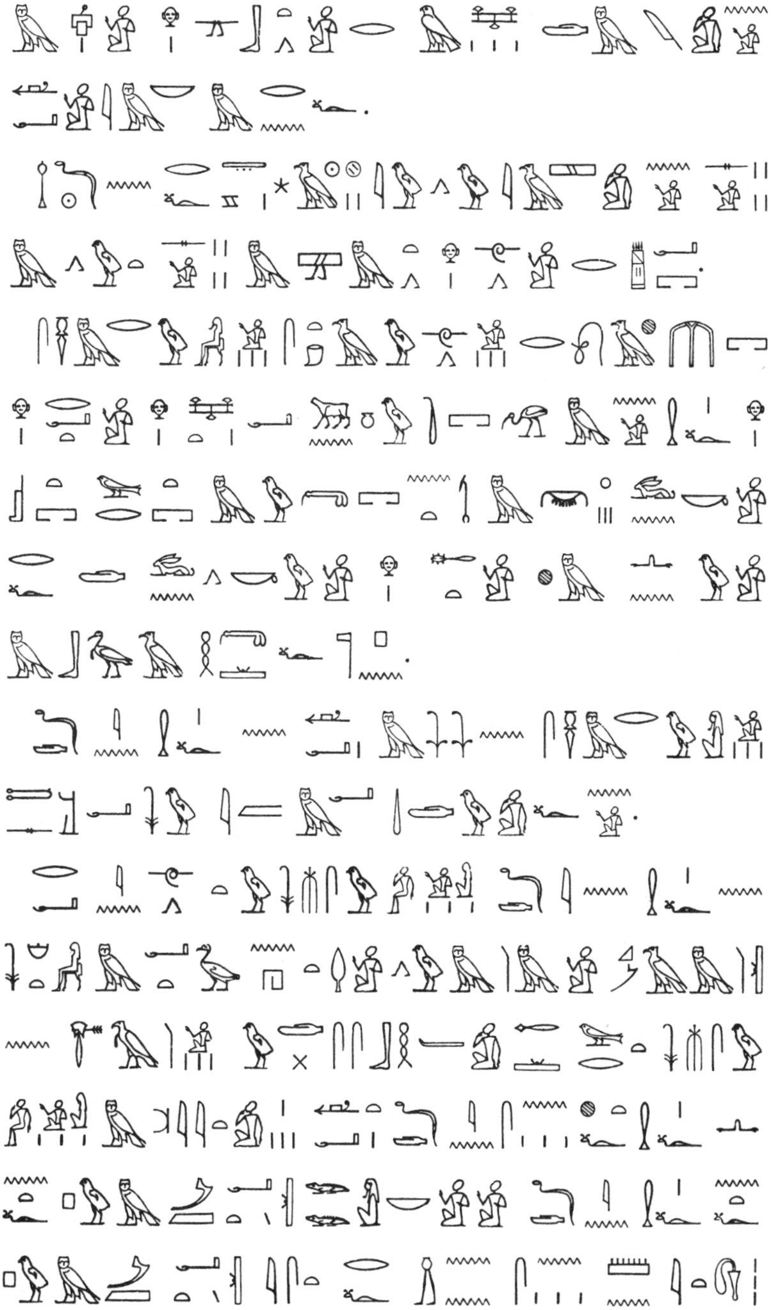

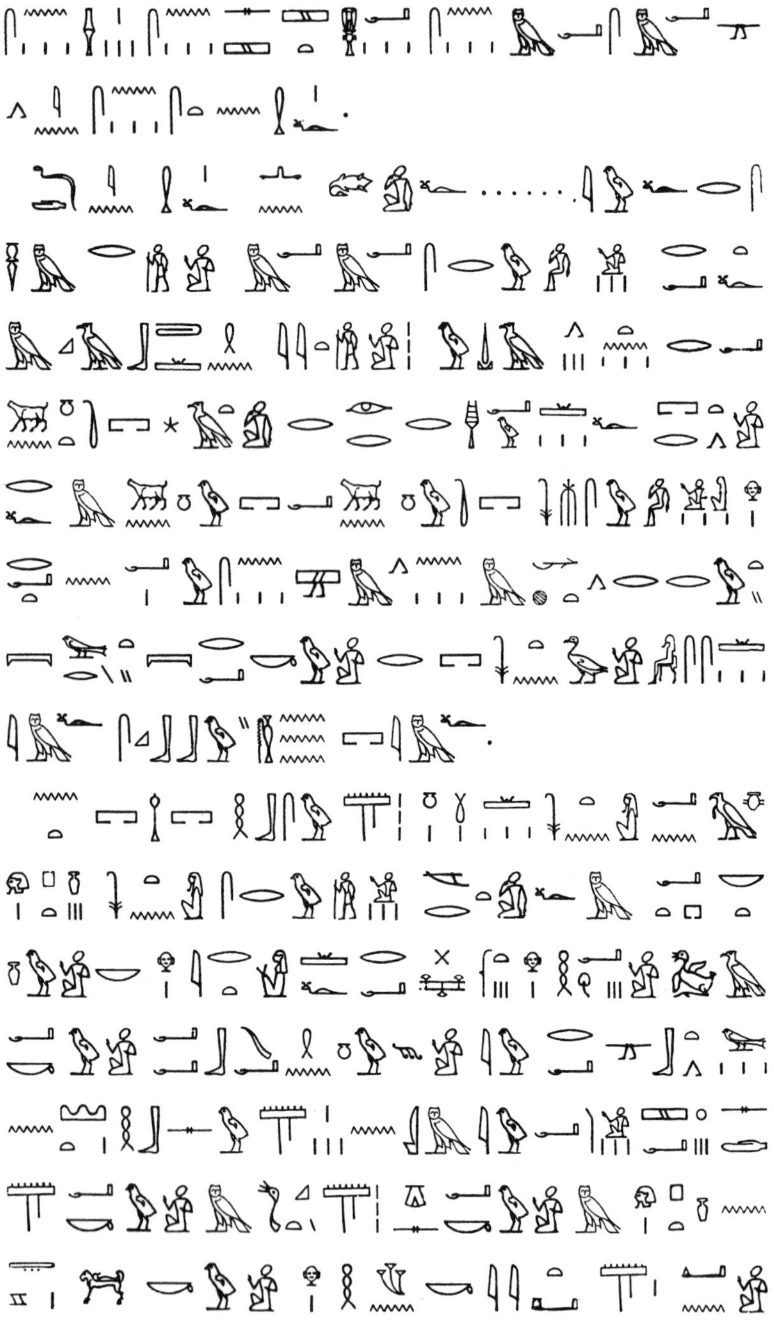

(GARDINER, *Die Erzählung des Sinuhe und die Hirtengeschichte*, Leipzig, 1909.)

VII

*The Tale of the Two Brothers**

* This later text is used because it illustrates the transition from Classical to New Egyptian.

3.

4.

5.

6.

7.

8. . .

9. (?)

10.

II. — I.

2.

3.

4.

5.

6.

7.

8.

9.

10.

III. — 1.

2.

3.

4.

5.

6.

. . . . . 7.

8.

. . . . . . 9.

10.

IV. — 1.

(?)

2.

(?) 3.

4.

5.

6.

7.

8.

9.

10.

V. — 1.

2.

3.

4.

5.

6.

7.

8.

9.

VI. — 1.

2.

3.

4.

5.

6.

7.

8.

9.

VII. — 1.

2.

3.

(?)

4.

5.

6.

7.

(sic) 8.

9.

VIII. — 1.

(sic)

2.

3.

4.

5.

6.

7.

8.

9.

IX. — 1.

2.

3.

4.

5.

6.

7.

8.

9.

X. — 1.

2.

3.

4.

5.

6.

7.

8.

9.

10.

XI. — 1.

2.

3.

4.

5.

6.

7.

8.

9.

10.

XII. — 1.

2.

3.

4.

5.

6.

7.

8.

9.

10.

XIII. — 1.

2.

3.

4.

5.

6.

7.

8.

9.

XIV. — 1.

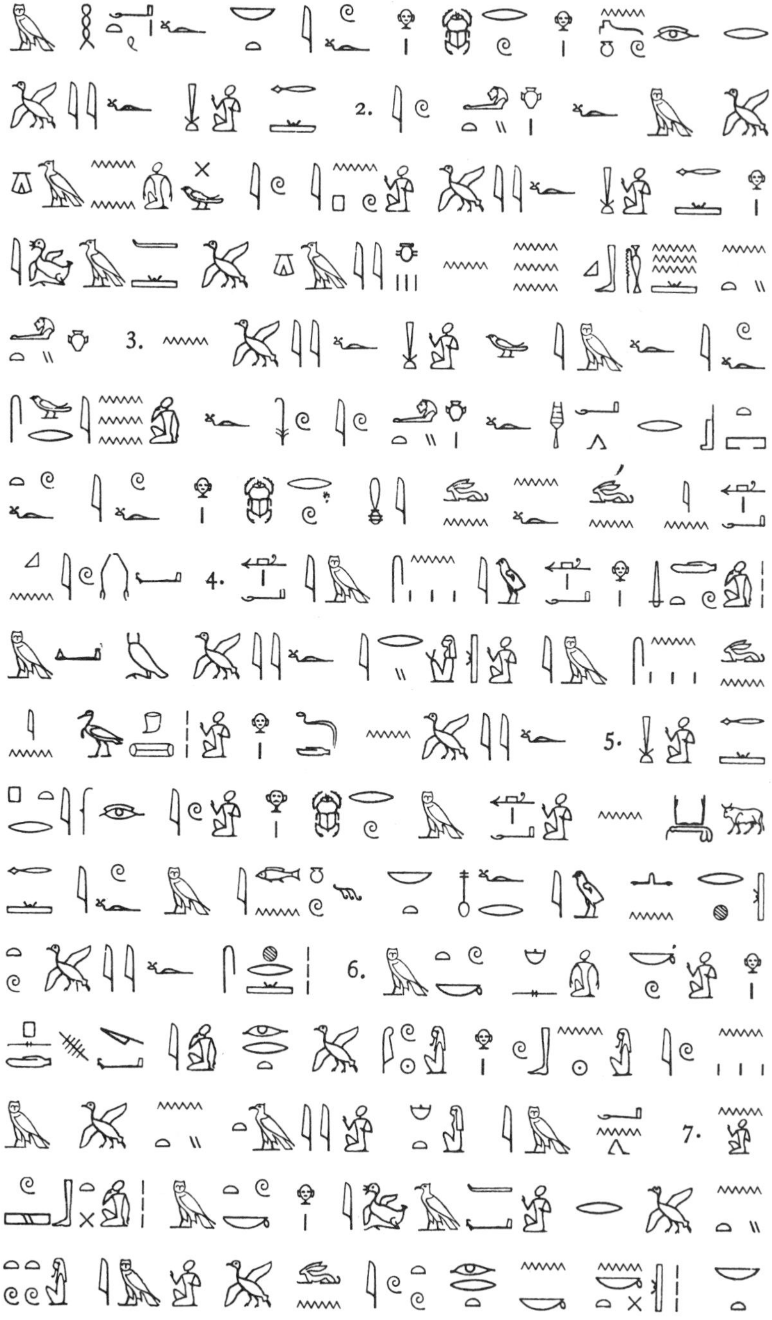

2.

3.

4.

5.

6.

7.

8.

9.

XV. — 1.

2.

3.

4.

5.

6.

7.

8.

9.

10.

XVI. — 1.

2.

3.

4.

5.

6.

7.

8.

9.

10.

XVII. — 1.

2.

3.

4.

5.

6.

7.

(?)

8.

9.

10.

XVIII. — 1.

2.

3.

4.

5.

6.

7.

8.

9.

10.

XIX. — 1.

2.

3.

4.

5.

......

6.

(BUDGE, *An Egyptian Reading Book,* 1896, pp. 1—40.)

SIGN LIST*

A. Men

2 det. "to call"; Interjection; *ʿš*

5 det. "to worship"; *dwꜣ, yꜣw*

8 det. "high," "to rejoice"; *ḳꜣy, ḥʿy, ḳꜣ, ḥʿ*

det. "to fall"

9 det. "to turn around"; *ʿny*

13 det. "to run"; phon. *yn*

15 det. "to dance," "to rejoice"; *kśy*

19 det. "to bow"; *kśy*

26 det. "dwarf"

27 det. "statue," "mummy," "figure," "death," *twt*

det. "mummy"

ḥwy "to strike"

29 *wr* "great"; *śr* (*śyr*?) "high official"; *śmśw* "old" (confused with 30)

30 det. "old"; *yꜣw, śmśw* (confused with 29)

31 det. "to smite"; *ḥw*

45 *nyny* "to pour a libation of water"

47 det. "to sow"

49 *ḳwś* "to build"

51 *ḳd* "to build"

56 *ḳś*

59 det. "statue"

70 det. "king"; *ʾyty* "king" (This figure means "king" also with other kinds of crowns or sceptres)

71 det. "child"; *ẖrd* and other words for "child"; *nn, ḥwn*, later *nw*

72 det. "to sit"

80, 79 det. "enemy," "death"; *ḫfty* "enemy"

---

* This Sign List is based upon ERMAN's selection in his *Ägyptische Grammatik*. The abbreviations used are: det. = determinative, phon. = phonogram (alphabetic or syllabic).

82 det. "soldier";
83 *mš*ʿ "soldier"

84 det. "prisoner," "barbarian"

85 det. "prisoner," "barbarian," "death"

88 det. "criminal"

89 det. "man"; suffix 1st pers. sing.

91 det. "to speak," "to think," "to eat," "to drink"

92 det. "to rest"; *wrd* "to rest"

93 det. *hn* "to adore"

94 det. *dw3* "to worship"; "to hide"

95 det. "to hide"; *ymn* "to hide"

98 *swr* "to drink"

"to row"

100 det. "to hide"; *ḥ3p*, *ymn* "to hide"; cf. O 48

101 *wʿb* "priest," "to clean"; cf. W 25

102 *s3ṯ* "to dispense water"

105 det. "to load," "to carry," "to build"; *3ṯp* "laden," *f3y* "to carry," *k3-t* "work"

106 *ḥḥ* (*n rnp·wt*) great number

110 det. "blessed dead"

113 det. "honoured person"; 1st pers. sing. suffix

117 det. "king" (also with different kinds of crowns and sceptres); suffix

120 "king," Osiris

128 *mynw* "shepherd," "watchman"; *s3w* "to watch"

"foreigner," Bedouin

129 *špsy* "honourable";
131 det. "blessed dead"

133 det. "to fall"; *ḫr*

135 det. "to swim"

B. Women

3 "singer," "dancer"

7 det. "woman"; suffix 1st and 2nd pers. sing.

9 det. "blessed dead"

10 det. "woman of position"

12 *yry* "belonging to"

14 det. "pregnant"; *bk3*

15 det. "to give birth to"; *mśy*

16 det. "nurse"; *rnn* "to rear"

C. Gods

1 *wśyr* Osiris

3, 4 *ptḥ* Ptaḥ

7 *ṯnn* Ptaḥ

9 *yn-ḥr·t* Onuris

10 *mnw* Min

11 *ymn* Amon

19 *šw* Show

25 *rᶜ* Reᶜ

27 *rᶜ* Reᶜ

31 *śtḫ* (*śtš*) Set; *bᶜr* Baal

32 *ynpw* Anubis

33 *ḏḥwty* Thot

36 *ḫnmw* Khnum

54 *m3ᶜ·t* Maāt; "truth"

D. Parts of Men

Cf. "teeth" V 4; "heart" W 23

1 *tp*, *ḏ3ḏ3* "head"; *tpy* "first"; det. "head," "to nod," *gw3*

3 *ḥr* "face"; "upon"; phon. *ḥr*

5 det. "hair," "temples," "colour," "bald," "grief"; *šn* "hair"; *wšr* "bald," "destroyed"

10 *yr·t* "eye"; *yr* "to see" (cf. *wśyr*); phon. *yr*; det. "to see," *ᶜn* (*ᶜyn*); *yry* "to do"

12 det. "eye," "to see"; det. *ᶜn* (*ᶜyn*)

13 det. "eye-paint"

14 det. "to weep"; *rmy* "weeping"

15 det. *ᶜn* (*ᶜyn*)

17 det. "divine eye"; *wḏ3·t*

cf. U 2

23 det. *mwt* "to die"; *yr* pupil; phon. *yr*

det. *m33* "to see"

25 det. "eye-brows"

28 *ḫnt* "nose," "before"; det. "nose," "breath," "joy"; *fnḏ* "nose"; *šr·t* "nose"; cf. F 4, 5

29 *r3* "mouth"; phon. *r3*, *r*

31 *śp·t* "lip"; *śpr* "rib," "to reach"; cf. N 28, 30

32 det. "jaw"

33 det. "to spit," "to flow out" (of the body)

35 *mdw* "staff," "to speak"

det. "back," *pśd*; *y3·t* "back"

37 late form of the preceding sign, and of the two following. Also *śm* for M 35

38 det. "to cut up" (cf. the preceding sign), *šʿ*

39 det. "breast," "to suckle"

41 *sẖn*, *ḥpt* "to embrace," "to happen"; det. "to embrace," *pgꜣ*

, *ḥm-kꜣ* "funerary-priest"

46 *kꜣ* "power," "strength," "force"; phon. *kꜣ*

47, 48, 42 *n* (*nn*), *nyw* "not"; *nywty* "not having"; phon. *n*; det. negation

49, 56 *ḏśr* "magnificent"

51 *ẖny* "to row"; phon. *ẖn*

52 *ʿḥꜣ*, *yḥꜣ* "to fight"; phon. *ʿḥꜣ*

58 *ḫwy* "to reign"

59 *ʿ* "arm"; *rdy* "to give"; phon. *ʿ*; det. for D 69 and D 63

60, 62 *mḥ* "ell"; *rmn* "arm"; *rmny* "to carry"; det. "arm," "what is done with the arm"; *grḥ*

63 *rdy*, *dy* "to give"; also used for the following

65 det. "to give"; phon. *my*

66 *ḥnk* "to present," "to distribute"

68 *yʿy* "to wash"

69 det. "that which requires power"; *nḫt* "strength"; "to smite"

72 *ḫrp* "to lead"

76 *ḏr·t* (*ḏꜣ·t*) "hand"; phon. *ḏ*

77 det. "hand"

79 *yꜣdy* "to tow"

82 det. "fist," "to fasten"; *ꜣmm* "to fasten"

84 *ḏbʿ* "finger"; *ḏbʿ* 10,000; cf. T 1 and 6

det. "middle," "correct," *mtr*; *ʿḳꜣ* "right"; *mtr* "middle," "sign"

87 det. "to take," "powder," "fruit"; *ṯꜣy* "to take"; *dḳr*

90 *bꜣḥ* "phallus," "before"; det. "male," "ox," "ass," "to copulate"; *ṯꜣ* "male"; *kꜣ* "ox"

phon. *mt* "man"

93 for Q 12 (T 12)

94 det. "testicles"

95 *ḥm·t* "woman"; phon. *ḥm*; cf. N 70

det. "female"

96 *yw* "to go," *nmt* "to pace"; det. "to go"; *ʿḳ* "to enter"

98 det. "to go back"; *ʿny* "to turn around"; *pry* "to go out"

99 det. "leg," "to step"; *rd* "foot"; *wʿr* "to flee"; phon. *gḥś*, *wʿr*

100 det. "to step over"; *thy* "to step over"

101 *grg* "to lie in wait for," "to equip," "lie"

102 phon. *ḳ*

det. "to eat"; *wnm* "to eat"

103 phon. *b*

109 det. "meat";
111 *ḥʿ* "limb";
ywf "meat"

E. Mammals

2 det. "horse"; *śśm·t*, *ḥtr* "horse"

3 det. "bull"; *yḥ* "ox"; *yw3* "ox"; *k3* "bull"

6 det. "cow"

9 "bound sacrificial animal"

12 det. "calf"; *bḥs* "calf"

13 det. *yb* "buck"; *yby* "to thirst"

14 det. "new-born animal"; phon. *yw*

15 *b3* "sacred ram"; *ẖnm* Khnum; *b3* "soul"; det. "ram"

17 det. "goat," "herd"; *m3-ḥḏ*?

19 *śʿḥ* "nobleman"

22 *ẖn·t* "leather skin"; *ẖnw* "interior"; phon. *ẖn*

28 det. *ḳnd* "to rage"; "baboon"

36 det. "lion"; *m3y* "lion"

38 phon. *rw*; later *šnʿ* for U 13

44 *nb* "sphinx"; det. "statue"

49 *s3b* "jackal"; *s3b* "judge"; det. *wp-w3·wt* Upwat

52 det. Anubis; *ynpw* Anubis

55 *ynpw* Anubis; later *ḥry-śšt3* (a title)

58 phon. *wn*

65 *śr* "giraffe"; *śr*

66
67 *śtš* (*śtẖ*) Seth; det. "dreadful"; "bad weather"; "ass"; *bʿr*

F. Parts of Mammals

Cf. "lungs" R 20; "tongue" S 37; "heart" Y 9, W 23. 46

3 *yḥ*, instead of E 3

4 wrong for D 28

5 "nose," "to breathe"; see D 28; also *rš*

6 det. "neck," "to swallow"

8 *šfy·t* "appearance"

11, 13 *šś3* "reasonable"

15 *pḥ·t* "power"; *3·t* "head-dress," "moment"

16 *ḥ3·t* "fore-part"; *ḥ3*

30 *3·t* "moment"; cf. F 15

33 *wp·t* "top," "summit"; phon. *wp*

35 *y3w·t* "office"

37 *wp-rnp·t* "New Year"

41 *ʿb* "horn"; phon. *ʿb*; det. "horn"; *db* "horn"

44 *ybḥ* "tooth"; phon. *bḥ*, *ḥw*, *by3*; det. "tooth," "activity of the mouth"

45 late for F 44

46 *mśdr* "ear"; *śdm* "to hear"; *ydn* "to represent"; det. "ear," "to hear"; *dng*, *yd*

48 *pḥ* "end," "to reach"; *kf3* "hinder part"; phon. *pḥ*

49 *ḫpš* "thigh," "strength"; det. "thigh"

52 *whm* "to repeat"; det. "leg of an animal"

whm "to repeat"

54 phon. *k3p*, *kp*; later for S 47

58 det. "beast"

59 *ś3b* "coloured"

60 *śty* "to shoot"

61 det. "tail," "thorn"

63 *ywʿ* "bone"; *ywʿ* "inheritance"; *yśwy* compensation; det. "meat"

G. Birds

1 phon. *3*, also for G 5

5 *tyw*

6, 7 phon. *nḥ*

8, 9 *ḥr*, *ḥrw* Horus; det. "falcon"

13 *ḥr-nb·ty* (?), royal title

15 det. "god," "king"

16 *ymn*; old for S 56

17 *ẖry·t-nṯr*; old for R 16

28 det. "holy bird"; *ʿḫm* "divine image"

30 *nr·t* "vulture"; *mw·t* Mut; *mw·t* "mother"; phon. *nr*, *mt*; det. "vulture"

31 *mw·t* Mut

33 *nb·ty* "the protective goddesses of Egypt"

36 phon. *m*

37 *mm*; late for Z 29

38, 39, 40 *my* "take"; *ym* "give"; phon. *m*

44 *mr*, *mt*

46 *gmy* "to find"; phon. *gm*

48 *ḏḥwty* Thot

53 *b3* "soul"; *bk* (*byk*) "to work"; phon. *b3*, *bk*

54 *b3w* "souls"

57, 58 *y3ḫ* "to shine"

60 det. *bnw* "phoenix"

61 *bʿḥ* "to overflow"

64 *dšr* "red"

63, 66 det. *wš3* "to feed"; *ḏf3* "food"; *ḥw*

67 det. "birds," "insects"; *s3* "son"; *3pd* "bird"; phon. *s3*; *gbb* Geb; det. *ḥtm*

rḫty "washer"

70 *śd3* "to tremble"

71 *ʿḳ* "to enter"

73 phon. *p3*; *p3y* "to flee"

75 *ḫny* "to flutter"; det. "to flee"; also for the following

det. *ḳm3*, *ṯn*; cf. T 6

78 *ḏb·t* "brick"

79 phon. *wr*; *wr* "great"

80 det. "small," "bad"; *nḏś* "small"; *šry* "small"

81, 82 *rḫy·t* "people"

83 phon. *w*

87 *ṯ3* "young bird"; phon. *ṯ3*

88 *sš* "nest"

90 *sš* "swamp," "nest"; *ywn* "nest"; det. "nest"

91 *śnḏ* "fear"

92 *b3* "soul"

H. Parts of Birds

1 old for G 67

3 *nr·t* "vulture"; *nr* "male"

5 det. *pḳ*

7 late for G 58

8 det. *mꜣʿ*

12 det. "to fly," "wing"

13 *šw·t* "feather"; phon. *šw*; det. "truth"; *mꜣʿ·t* "truth"

17 see D 62

18 *šꜣ·t* "bird-claw"?

20 for D 84

21 later *sꜣ* "son"; det. "goddess," "queen"

I. Amphibia

2 *ʿšꜣ* "many"

4 det. "crocodile"; *ꜣd* "fury"

yty "king"

det. *śꜣḳ*

7 *śbk* Sobk

8 } *km* "black"; phon. *km*

9 det. "frog"; goddess *ḥḳt*

10 *ḥfn* "tadpole"; *ḥfn* 100,000

11 | det. "snake"; "goddess"

16 |

22 det. "worm"

24 det. "evil being"

26 *ḏ·t* "serpent," "snake"; *ḏ·t* "body"; phon. *ḏ*

27 see Z 9

30 phon. *f*

32 later *pry* "to come out"

33 later *ʿḳ* "to go in"

K. Fish

1 phon. *yn*; *rm* "fish"

ʿnḏ-mr(?) "government title"

4 det. "fish," "disgust"; *bś* "lead in"

6 *spꜣ*

10 *ḫꜣ·t* "body"; phon. *ḫꜣ*

L. Insects

Cf. "mussel" N 72

1 *by·t* "bee," "honey"; *byty* "king of Lower Egypt"

4 *ḫpr* "beetle"; *ḫpr* "to become"

5 det. "flying-sun"

7 *ʿff* "fly"

8 det. "chastity"

9 "scorpion," *śrḳ* "to breathe"; goddess *śrḳ·t*

see I 30

M. Plants

Cf. bundle of reeds Q 32; D 37

1 *y3m* "a tree," "sweet"; det. "tree"; *ḳb*

det. "tree"

9 *ḫt* "wood," "tree"; phon. *ḫt*; det. "wood," "tree"

13 *rnp·t* "year"; *tr* "time"; *ḥ3·t-sp* "year of a reign"; *rnp* "to bloom"; cf. M 15. 17

15 *tr* "time"; det. *ty*, *mry*; cf. 13

16 *rnp·t* "year"; cf. 13

17 *rnp* "to bloom"; cf. 13

22 *nḫb* "leaf"; goddess *Nḫb·t*; city *Nḫb* (el Kab)

phon. *nn*

24 *nswt* (*ny-św t*?), "king of Upper Egypt"; *rś* "south"; phon. *św*

24
30 *rś* "south"

26
27 *šmᶜ* Upper Egypt; "to practice music"

33 phon. *y*

y, *yy*

34 *yy* "to go"

35 *śḫ·t* "field"; *śm* (cf. D 37)

36 *ᶜ3b·t* "offering"

37 *š3* "field"; *3ḫ·t* "inundation"; phon. *š3*

41 phon. *ḥn*; *ysy* "old"; det. "plant"

42 det. "swamp," "north"; phon. *ḥ3*

43 det. "swamp," "north"; *ydḥ* "Delta swamps"; *mḥ·t* "north"

45 det. Upper Egypt

47
48 *w3ḏ* "green"; phon. *w3ḏ* (later *wḏ*)

50
47 late for N 39

58 det. "buds"

59 for V 39

63 det. "flower"

67 phon. *wn*; *wnm* "to eat"; cf. R 28

wn-ḏw

68 *ḫ3* 1000; phon. *ḫ3*

70 later form of ; cf. V 6

74, 75, 76 — *ḥḏ* "club," "white"; phon. *ḥḏ*; also for the following

77 old, 73 late — *wḏy* "to command"; phon. *wḏ*

U 32, 79 — *ḥśf* "to ward off"

80 *mśy* "to give birth to," phon. *mś*

82 *bd·t* "spelt"

84 det. "ear of corn"

86 *yt* "barley"

89, 88 — *šnw·t* "barn"

90 det. "wine"

93, 94 — *bnr* "sweet"; "date"; *rd* "to grow"

98 *nḏm* "sweet"

N. Heaven, Earth, Water

1 *p·t* "heaven"; *ḥr·t* "heaven"; *ḥry* "that which is above"; det. "heaven," "above"; *h3y·t* "hall"

2, 3 — det. "night," "evening"; *grḥ* "night"

4 det. "rain," "dew"; *y3d·t* "dew"

5 *tḥn* "lightening," "to shine"; det. "weather," "rain"

7 *rʿ* "sun," "sun-god"; det. "sun," "time"; *hrw* day; *śśw* "day of the month"

8 see Z 11

11 *rʿ* "sun" (as god)

13 *ḥnmm·t* "mankind"; det. "rays"; *wbn* "to make light"

14 *śpd·t* triangle; *śpd* "make ready"; *śpd·t* "dog-star"

17 det. "flying-sun"

23 *ḫʿy* "to rise"; phon. *ḫʿ*

26 see X 12

28 *šsp* "span"

28, 30 — *yʿḥ* "moon"; *ybd* "month"; cf. D 31

ybd "month"

35 *śb3* "star"; *dw3* "morning-star"; *dw3·t* "underworld"; *dw3* "to adore"; *wnwt* "hour"; phon. *śb3*, *dw3*

36 late *dw3·t* "underworld"

37 *t3* "land"; phon. *t3*; det. *ḏ·t*

39 *t3wy* "the two Egypts"

40 *ḫꜣś·t* "foreign country"; *smy·t* "desert," "necropolis"; god *ḫꜣ*; det. "desert," "foreign country"

42 *ḏw* "mountain"; phon. *ḏw*; later *mn*

44 *ꜣḫ·t* "horizon"

46 *śpꜣ·t* "district"; *ḥsp* "district"; det. "section of country"

47 det. "land"

X 21 det. "land"; *ydb* "bank"

48 det. "land," "limited time"

49 *wꜣ·t* "way"; det. *wꜣy* "to be far"; "way"; "place"; *mṯn* "way"; phon. *wꜣ*, *ḥr*

śwꜣ "to go by"

50 *gś* "side"; phon. *ym*, *gś*; later *m*

51, 52 det. "stone"; *ynr* "stone"

53 det. "grain" (of sand, seed, &c.)

55 phon. *n*

mw "water"; phon. *mw*; det. "water"

58 *mr* "canal"; *mry* "to love"; phon. *my*; det. "waters"; cf. N 66

62, 59, 60 *š* "sea"; phon. *š*; det. "sea," "water"; *ḫnt*

for the preceding, and for 58

61 *šm* "to go"

66 *yw* "island"; *ꜣḫ·t* "horizon"; phon. *yw*; det. "island"

"bread," cf. X 1

Z 20 *sny* "to open," "to pass by," *sn* "similar"

67 *ꜣḫty* "belonging to the horizon"

70 det. *byꜣ*; cf. D 95

72 phon. *ḫꜣ*

O. Buildings and their Parts

Cf. "pillar" Q 29. T 41

1 *n·t* "city"; det. "city"

3, 4 *pr* "house"; *pry* "to go out"; phon. *pr*; det. "building"

6 *pr·t-r-ḫrw* "funeral-offering"

7 *pr-ḥḏ* "treasury"

9 phon. *h*

10 *mr* name of Egypt; phon. *mr*, *nm*

12, 22 *ḥ·t* "large house"

15 *ḥ·t nṯr* "temple"

16 *ḥ·t ꜥꜣ·t* "castle"

17 *nb·t-ḥ·t* Nephthys

19 *ḥ·t-ḥr* Hathor

29 ʿḥʿ "palace"

32 wśḫ·t "palace court"

36 det. "wall"; ynb "wall"

37 det. "to destroy"

41 det. "fortress"

43 det. "gate"

44 ṯ3yty title of the Chief Justice

45 ḳnb "angle"; ḳnb·t "officials"

48, U49 ḥ3p "to hide"; phon. ḥ3p, ḥp; cf. A 100

52 det. "pyramid," "grave"

53 det. "obelisk"; tḫn "obelisk"

54 det. "memorial tablet"; wḏ "stela"

61 ḫkr "to adorn"; cf. X 19

62 sḥ "arbour," "hall"; sḥ "counsel"; det. "hall"; later for the following sign

ʿrḳ "to bend"

63, 64 ḥb-śd "royal jubilee"

65 ḥb "feast"; cf. 63 and W 49

68, 67 det. "stairs," "to ascend"

69 ʿ3 "door"; det. "to open"; phon. ʿ3

70 phon. s

71 swy (?) "to go"; sby "to go," "to bring"; ms "to bring"

73 ṯsy "to knot"; phon. ṯs

74 mnw Min; ḫm "holy of holies"

75 mnw Min

77, Q34 phon. ḳd

80 sḥ "hall"

P. Ships and their Parts

1 det. "ship," "to journey"; wy3; ḫd "to move down stream"

det. pnʿ "to turn over"

6 wḥʿ

14 det. "to sail"; ḫnty "to sail up stream"

16 ṯ3w "wind," nf, nfw "breath"; det. "wind," "air"

19 ʿḥʿ "to stand"; phon. ʿḥʿ

21 det. "rudder"; ḥm "rudder"

22 ḫrw "voice"; ḥp·t; det. "rudder"

23 šsp (sšp, later šp) "to receive"; phon. šsp (sšp, šp)

Q. House Articles

1 ś·t "seat"; 3ś; 3ś·t Isis (cf. wśyr); phon. ś, ḥtm

3 det. "armchair"

5 wṯs "portable chair"; phon. wś; det. "chair"

7, 8 det. "to lie," "to sleep," "to die"; śḏr "at night"

9 phon. ś

ḫmnw "eight"

12 for T 12

15 $\frac{2}{3}$

17 ḥtp "offering"; ḥtp "to rest"

wdḥw "table for food"

20 ḫr "under"

ḫr·t-hrw "daily"

23, 25 det. "coffin"; ḳrśw "coffin"

26 y3·t "place"

28 ḏb3 "to repair"; phon. ḏb3

29 ywn "pillar"; phon. ywn; later yn

31 phon. ḫn

32, 34 phon. ys

37 god šsm

39 mḏr (later mḏd) "to press"

42 det. "clothes"; mnḫ·t + šś (ᶜrf V 6–8)

mnḫ·t "clothes"

44 det. wrś "pillow"

46 śry·t "standard"

47 det. "shade"; ḫ3b·t "shade"

48 det. "balances"

51, 52 wḏᶜ "to set right"

53, 54 wṯs, ṯsy, ṯs "to lift up"; det. ṯs; cf. T 2

58 m3ᶜ "true"

59 stand for images of gods and for district names; cf. G 15. 48, O 75

60 phon. p

R. Temple Articles

Cf. F 35, S 47

1 wdḥw

2 det. "altar"; ḫ3w·t "altar"

13 *nṯr* "god"; det. "god"

16 *ḫry·t-nṯr* "kingdom of the dead"

18 *ḏd* "holy pillar," "to remain"

20 *smꜣ* "lungs," "to unite"

22 *śn* "two," "brother"; phon. *śn*

26 *yꜣb* "left"; cf. U 31

28 *ymy* "to consist in"; for M 67 in *wnm* "to eat"; phon. *ym*

M 67

29 *śšꜣ·t* "goddess of wisdom"

S. Clothing, Jewelry, Insignia

Cf. Y 11, M 80

1, 24 "wreath"; *mḥ* "wreath"; cf. T 7

3 later phon. *k*

7 *ḫprš* "head-dress"

8 *ḥḏ·t* "crown of Upper Egypt"

11 *n·t* "crown of Lower Egypt," *dšr·t* the same; *byty* "king of Lower Egypt"; phon. later *n*

13 det. *śḫm·t* "crown of Upper and Lower Egypt"

14 see V 1

17 *šw·ty* "feather as head-dress"

28 *yḥwty* "farmer"; phon. *ʿḥ*, *yḥ*

30 det. "skirt"; *šnḏw·t* "skirt"

31 *śṯy·t* name of a country; goddess Sathis; *śṯ*

32, Q 13 det. "clothes"; *ḥbś* "clothes"

37 *nś* "tongue"; *ymy-rꜣ* "foreman"; "death"; phon. *nś*, *mr*

38 *ṯb·t* "sandal"

39 *šn* "circle"; cf. 44

41 *dmḏ* "to unite"

42 Isis

43 *ʿnḫ* "to live"

44 *ḏꜣś·t* (?) "treasure"; det. "seal"; *ḫtm* "seal"

45 *ḏꜣś·t* (?) "treasure"; gentilic: "treasurer"

46 *mny·t* "weight on collar"

47 *kꜣp* "to smoke"; phon. *kꜣp*, *kp*; cf. F 54

ʿ "caravan"

48 *ʿpr* "to provide"; det. "tassel"

50 *śhm* "mighty"; *ḫrp* "to lead"; *ʿb3* "sceptre"

m-n "to take"

56 *ymn* "right," *ymn·t* "western," *wnmy* "right"

60 *ḫw·t* "fan"

62 *ḥḳ3* "to rule"

63 *ʿw·t* "sheep," "pigs," &c.

64 *w3ś·t* "sceptre"; *dʿm* "gold"; *w3ś*, *dʿm*; cf. U 54

65 *w3ś·t* Thebes

66 *wśr* "strong"

75 *nḫ3ḫ3*

76 god *b3b3*

T. Arms and War Articles

Cf. M 74–76; U 45, 38; R 22; V 27; Z 29, 30

6, 1 det. "foreign"; *ʿ3m* "Asiatic," *ṯḥn* "Libyan," *nḥśy* "negro"; *dʿ*; *ḳm3* "to throw," "to create"; *ṯny* "to lift up oneself"; cf. G 75, T 2, 13, S 63

2 *rś* "to grow"

3 *sḫn* "support"

7 *mdḥ* "to cut"; det. "axe"

9 *tpy* "first"

10 *ḫpš* "crescent-sword"

12, 20 *śšm* "butcher"; *śšm* "to lead"; cf. Q 12, D 93

13 det. *mny* "to land," "to graze"

14, 15 det. "to cut"; *dm* "to sharpen," "to name"

21 *pḏ·t* "bow"; det. "bow"

26, 31 *sty* Nubia

28 *pḏ·t* "bow"; *pḏ* "to broaden out"

33 *śšr* "arrow"; *śḫr* "to milk," *swn*

38 *ś3* "back," "behind"; phon. *ś3*

41 *ʿ3* "great"; phon. *ʿ3*

43 *ḫ·t*, *ḫ3·t* "body"; phon. *ḫ*

45 det. "war-chariot"; *wrry·t* "war-chariot"

U. Tools and Agricultural Implements

Cf. M 79; V 15; W 6; X 17

1 ḫnr "to confine"

late for *m*

2 *ty·t* "part"; cf. D 17

3 *śtp* "to select"

5, 4 } phon. *nw*

7 det. "to smite"; *ḥwy* "to smite"

8 phon. *m3*

m3ʿ

12 } *mry* "to love"; phon. *mr*; det. "to hoe"

šnʿ "to ward off"; "warehouse"

13 *hb* "plough"; *pr·t* "fruit"; phon. *hb*; det. "to plough"; also for the preceding *šnʿ*

14 *tm* "to complete"; *ytm* Atum; phon. *tm*

} *by3* "ore," "to be astonished"

18 *ḥḳ3* corn-measure

19 phon. *ty*

20 det. "weight," "mineral"; *śmn*; *ḥsmn* "a metal," "natron"

21 phon. *ḏ3*

24 *mr* "sick," "pyramid"; phon. *mr*; *3b* (U 31)

27 *mnḫ* "to saw," "excellent"

28 *ḥm* "handwork"

29 *wb3* "to open"

31 phon. *3b*

32 see M 79, *ḥśf*

36, 35 } *nḏ* "to paint"

38, 37 } *wʿ* "one"; phon. *wʿ*

40, V 20 } *nrt* Neith

41 det. "to sheer"

42 *šmś* "to follow"

45 *ḳś* (*ḳrś*?) "bone"; *ḳrś* "to bury"; phon. *ḳś*, *ḳrś*; det. "bone"; "tube"; *gnw·t*

mśnty (?) "sculptor"

47 see V 4

48 *ś3ḥ*

49 see O 48; *ḥp* (*ḥ3p*)

50 *nb* "gold"

53 *ḥḏ* "silver"

54 *ḏʿm* "gold"

55 *śḫt* "net"

śḫt "to weave"

V. Wicker-work

Cf. M 77, 73; O 73; Q 9

1 det. "cord"; *šnṯ*; *š3·t* "hundred"; "to fasten"; phon. late *w*; cf. S 14

2 *śṯ3* "to draw"; det. *3ś*

4, U 47 *ś3ḥ* "toe," "to land"

5 phon. *3w*; *3wy* "wide"

ym3ḫ "dignity"

6 phon. *šś*; det. "cord," "to bind"; cf. V 8

wg3

phon. *šn*; cf. M 70

8 det. "sack"; *ʿrf* "bag"; phon. *gb*

10 det. "to bind," "to loose"; "book"; *ʿrḳ* "to end"

13 late for V 10

15, 18 *mḥ* "to fill"; phon. *mḥ*

17 *šd* "to take"; phon. *šd*

20 see U 40

21 *ʿnd* (*ʿ3ḏ*?) "to be well"; phon. *ʿnḏ* (*ʿ3ḏ*?)

25 *śnṯ* "foundation"

26 phon. *w3*

27 *rwḏ* (*rḏ*) "to grow"; det. *3y*, *3r*

28 *s3* "protection"

29 *s3* "protection"

30 phon. *ḥ*

34 phon. *śk*; cf. V 38

37 *w3ḥ* "to lay"; cf. V 38

38 for V 34, 37

39, 40 *wdn* "offering"; cf. M 59

41 *pḫr* "to surround"; *dbn* "to surround," "weight"; *wḏb* "to turn back"; *ḳ3b* "interior"

43 phon. *ṯ*

44 *yṯy* "to seize"

45 *wt* "to wrap up"; det. "to embalm," "death," "smell," "to reckon"; *ḥśb* "to reckon"; cf. Y 3

46 det. "smell"

W. Vessels

Cf. V 8; E 22; V 17

1 *b3ś·t* name of a city; goddess Bast; det. "oil"; *mrḥ·t* "oil"

4 *ḥsy* “to praise”

5 det. “cold”; *ḳbb*, *ḳbḥ* “to be cool”

6 *ḥm* “majesty,” “servant”

8
9 *ḫnt* “before”

11 *ḫnm* “to unite”; Khnum

13
23
17
21 det. “vessel,” “liquid”; *ḥḳ·t* “beer”; *dpw*; *wb3* “servant”

14 det. “milk”

20 det. “wine”

21 phon. *nw*, *yn* (?); det. *ḳd*, *nḏ*; “vessel,” “liquid”; *ḫnw* “interior”

22 *yny* “to bring”; phon. *yn*

23 *yb* “heart”; det. “heart”

det. “stone vessel,” “ivory”; *m3wṯ*

25 *wʿb* “clean,” “priest”; cf. A 101

27 *ʿb*, *wʿb* “clean”

29 *my* (old *mr*) “as,” “like”; phon. *my*

31 *wśḫ* “wide”; *ḥnw·t* “lady”; phon. *ʿb*; det. “vessel”

33 see X 1

38
37 det. “fire”; *nśr*

39 *b3*

40 *ḏr* “border”; phon. *ḏr*

42 *nś·t* “throne”; phon. *g*

43 *nb* “lord,” “all”; phon. *nb*

44 phon. *k*

46 *k3·t* “female beast”

49 det. “feast”; *ḥb* “feast”; cf. O 65

50 *ḫry-ḥb* “priest”

53 *yt* “barley,” “corn-measure”; det. “grain”

Z 27 late for 53

57 *ydr* “flock”

59 *ḥmt* “copper”; det. “metal”

60 *t3* “hot”; phon. *t3*

X. Offerings

1
N 66 det. “bread”

3 *nḫn* el Kab

W 35
W 33
5
19 *t3* “bread”; phon. *t3*; *yt* “father”

10
11 *p3w·t* “bread for offering”; *p3w·t* “antiquity”; det. “bread”

N 26		} *pśḏ·t* "ninefold"
12		
14		*sp* "heap of corn"; *sp* "times"; cf. 3
15		old form of 14
17		phon. *ẖ*
21		cf. N 47
22		*rdy* "to give"

Y. Writing, Music, and Game Articles

1		*sẖ* (*sš*) "to write"; *nᶜᶜ* "mottled"; *śnᶜᶜ* "to polish"
2		*mḏȝ·t* "book"; det. abstract idea; *dmḏ* "together"
3		*gȝw* "sack"; *mśn*; det. *gȝw*
8		} *sšš·t* "sistrum," "clapper"; cf. S 50 *śẖm*
6		
9		*nfr* "good"
11		*śyȝ* "to recognize"
12		*mn* "to remain"; phon. *mn*
14		*ybȝ* man at draughts

Z. Strokes and Doubtful Signs

5		} determinative of the dual; phon. *y*
7		} det. "to divide," "to reckon," "to break"; *šbn* "to be different"; *śwȝ* "to go by"; cf. N 49
9		*mḏ* "ten"
I 27		*mḏ·t* "depth"
10		} det. "furniture," "basket"; *ḥry·t* "fear"
11		*dny*; det. "to divide"
N 8		det. "circle"; *ḳd*
12		phon. *t*
15		*ḳn* "to finish"; det. *ḏȝḏȝ·t*
19		"cartouche"; *rn* "name"
20		see N 66
22		*śḳr* "to smite"
25		*yp·t* "harem"
29		} phon. *nm*
30		

GLOSSARY

ꜣ

ꜣw length.
ꜣwy to be long, to be wide, to be happy, glad.
ꜣwy-yb to make glad.
ꜣw·t length.
ꜣw·t-ʿ present, gift.
ꜣb to cease.
ꜣby to desire, to wish, to love.
ꜣby (*ꜣbw*) panther.
ꜣbẖ (*y*?) to mix.
ꜣbd hen.
ꜣbḏw city of Abydos.
ꜣpd goose, duck, fowl.
ꜣmm to grasp, to hold.
ꜣh to consent, to be beautiful.
ꜣḥ·t land, field, estate.
ꜣẖ glorious.
ꜣẖw splendour, the blessed ones.
ꜣẖ·t glory, horizon; two horizons as title of Harmachis.
ꜣśy to hasten.
ꜣśy·w quickly.
ꜣś·t goddess Isis.
ꜣś·t place.
ꜣś·t-ḥr direction.
ꜣšr to roast.
ꜣḳ to diminish.
ꜣgby flood.
ꜣ·t moment.
ꜣtp (*ꜣṯp*) to fill, to load.
ꜣḏꜣ splinter.

y

y Oh! behold, he who, that which.
yꜣꜣ name of a district.
yꜣꜣy·t branch.
yꜣw worship, adoration, to praise.
yꜣwy old age.
yꜣw·t office, a noble, old man; cattle.
yꜣb·ty eastern.
yꜣrr·t fruit, grapes, wine.
yꜣẖw glorified, profitable.
yꜣẖ·t horizon.
yꜣš to call, to summons.
yꜣk·t herb, bulblike.
yꜣ·t place, holy place.
yy to come.
yy-wy welcome!
yywyꜣ father of Queen Tiy.
yʿy to wash.
yʿḥmś Ahmose.
yw to come, to go, to arrive, to travel; and, but, for, then, when; island; dog.
ywꜣ cow.
ywy I; to separate.
ywʿ to reward, heir.
ywʿw inheritance.
ywf meat.
yw·f he.
ywnw Heliopolis.
ywr conception.
ywh to take.
yw (*t*) to come.
yw·tw one, he, she, it; there is, there was; with det. of deity = Pharaoh.
ywtn ground, mud.
yb heart; to think, to believe.
yb-yʿy restorer.
ybḥ tooth.
ybd month.

yp to count; grief.
ypd plank (?).
yf (*ywf*) meat.
yfd linen.
yfdy bed.
ym = *m*; in, to, there, therefore.
ym river, sea.
ymꜣ tent.
ymꜣḫ honour, reputation, worthy.
ymꜣḫy worthy.
ymy to give, to put, to make, to allow; come!; be not; during, in.
ymy-ḥꜣ·t old time.
ymy·t during, in.
ymn god Amon.
ymn-mś Amenmes.
ymn·ty west, western, right.
ymnt·t western.
ymr to be deaf.
ym(?)·*t* graciousness.
yn by, when, is not?, pray!, "said he," introduces a question.
yny to bring, to summons, to take, to take possession.
ynw gifts, offerings.
ynb wall.
ynpw god Anubis; name of a person.
yn-m who?
ynnꜣ name of a person.
ynr stone, shell.
yn-rf therefore.
ynḥ to surround, to enclose; eyebrow.
yn·t fish; valley.
yntf Intef.
(*y*) *nḏ-ḥr* hail!; homage, praise.
yr now.
yry to do, to make; belonging to, of such a nature, companion.
yry-yḫ·t offerings.
yry-ʿ·t officer.
yry-mʿw with, in company with.
yry-ḥꜣ·t pilot.
yrp wine, beer.
yr-pꜣ verily.
yr̥ = *r* to, than.
yrnṯ river Orontes.
yr·t eye.
yrṯ·t milk.
yhw (*yhy·t*) stable.
yhm·t bank (of a river).
yḥ cow, ox.
yḥw weakness, childishness.
yḫ how!, what?, Ah!, let me.
yḫm (*ḫm*) not to know.
yḫ·t thing; wealth, goods.
yḫ-tm lest.
ys to go.
ysy hasten.
yś behold, that (particle), interrogative.
yśr tamarisk; *yśry* belonging to the tamarisk.
yśśy Isosi.
yś·t place.
yśt behold.
yśtn to surround.
yśtw behold.
yśtw-yr whilst.
yś·t-r·f now, therefore.
yḳ beef.
yḳr to be wise, to be fine, exceedingly.
yt = *ytf* = *tf* father; corn, barley, grain.
yty to take; king, prince.
ytm god Atum.
ytn to quarrel with.
yt-nṯr "father of the god" = title of a priest.
ytrw stream.
ytḥ to drag.
yṯꜣ to carry off, to lead, to take away; thief, crooked.
yṯy to take, to take to, to seize.

yṯn sun; Aton.
ydb·wy two borders.
ydnw assistant of.

ꜥ

ꜥ arm, hand, side, place.
ꜥꜣ ass, door, here, great.
ꜥꜣy to be great, to beat.
ꜥꜣ·w very much.
ꜥꜣb to be astonished (?)
ꜥꜣm Asiatic, Syrian.
ꜥꜣ-ḫpr·w-rꜥ Thutmose III.
ꜥyn lime-stone.
ꜥꜥy to speak, to utter a cry, foreign language.
ꜥꜥb to comb.
ꜥwꜣ to decay, to stink; to steal.
ꜥwꜣy to steal, to rob; robber; to harvest.
ꜥwn-yb caprice.
ꜥw·t-ḫꜣś·t game.
ꜥb horn.
ꜥbꜣ sceptre.
ꜥbt (*ḥb*) feast.
ꜥfn·t hair.
ꜥm to understand, to give heed; to absorb, to devour.
ꜥmwynnsy name of a person.
ꜥn again.
ꜥny to return, to retreat, to repeat, to turn around, to look around.
ꜥnḫ to live, life.
ꜥnḫwy ears.
ꜥntyw perfumes.
ꜥrf bag.
ꜥrrw·t office of administration.
ꜥrḳ to swear an oath.
ꜥrḳy last.
ꜥḥꜣ to fight, strife, combat.
ꜥḥꜣw weapon, shaft.
ꜥḥꜣwty combat.
ꜥḥꜥ to stand; then; palace; cargo-boat; life, time of life, duration of life.
ꜥḥꜥw time; rank.
ꜥhꜥ·t grave.
ꜥẖnwty royal chamber or cabinet.
ꜥš to call, to cry; cedar.
ꜥšꜣ to be many, numerous.
ꜥḳ to enter, to come to.
ꜥḳw food, bread.
ꜥ·t door, chamber; limb, member of body.
ꜥḏꜣ evil, evil-doer, violence.
ꜥḏy fat, greece.
ꜥḏd young man.
ꜥḏd·t young woman.

w

w (?) place, district.
wꜣy to bow, to be inclined to, to be about to.
wꜣy-r to be far from.
wꜣw wave.
wꜣb persea (tree)?
wꜣḥ to place, to set, to lie down, to lay down, to last; to be happy; fortunate.
wꜣḫ hypostyle hall.
wꜣḫy hall, pillared hall, hypostyle hall.
wꜣś sceptre; happiness, good fortune.
wꜣśy to go to ruin, to be decayed.
wꜣś·t Thebes.
wꜣgy to make festival.
wꜣ·t way, road, side.
wꜣ·t-ḥr name of a place.
wꜣḏ to be green, green, young.
wꜣḏ-wr sea.
wꜥ one.
wꜥb to be clean, clean; priest; to purify, purification.

wʿb·t place of purification.
wʿf to fetter, to bind.
wʿ-nb each one.
wʿr to come out.
wʿr·t coffer.
wʿ·t sole.
wʿ·ty sole, only, altogether.
wbꜣ to enter.
wbꜣ·t servant.
wbn to rise, to arise.
wpy to judge, to plead, to open.
wpw (*ypw*) messenger.
wp-wꜣ·wt god Upuat, title of Osiris.
wpw-ḥr except.
wpw·t (*ypw·t*) messenger, work, knowledge, tidings, report.
wmt·t room.
wn to open.
wny name of a person.
wnw·t hour.
wnm (*wm*) to eat, food.
wn-pꜣ when.
wnn existence, lifetime.
wnn-nfr Osiris.
wnḫ to clothe, to put on, to tie up (hair).
wr to be great, great, prince, chief, oldest (son); evil.
wrry·t war-chariot.
wrḥ to anoint, to smear, to daub.
wrš to pass time, to watch; by day.
wršy·t watchman.
wrḏ to rest.
whn to renew, to report.
wḥy·t tribe.
wḥʿ to return home.
wḫꜣ to seek; to shake out, to fall.
wśyr Osiris.
wśm electrum.
wśr to be mighty, mighty, wisdom.
wśr-rf a proper name.
wśḫ to be wide, width.
wśḫ·t punt, ferry, raft.
wšb to reply, answer.
wgꜣ evil, shame, feebleness.
w·t name of a town.
wtṯ to beget.
wdy to utter.
wdn to make offerings, offering.
wdḥw libation table.
wḏ to command, to entrust.
wḏꜣ to go, to pass away, to come; to be well, to be whole, to be happy, to be glad; good fortune.
wḏʿ to cut off; divorced person.
wḏw garland.
wḏb shore.
wḏf to delay.

b

bꜣ to be happy, fortunate; to hack up.
bꜣw might.
bꜣḳ oil.
bꜣk servant.
bꜣ·t bush, stalk.
bꜣtꜣw name of a person.
byꜣ fortress; mine in Sinai.
byꜣy·t a wonder, miracle.
byꜣ·t character, person.
byn evil.
byk to work, servant.
by·t honey.
byty-dꜣs·t high official who carries the seal of the king.
bʿl god Baal.
bʿḥ to flood.
bw place; not.

bw-nb all men, everyone.
bw-n-rꜣ "place of the mouth" = outside.
bw ẖr place at which.
bb·t (*bꜣbꜣ·t*) whirlpool (?).
bn not.
bnw·t black granite.
bnr sweet.
bn·t harp.
bhꜣ to flee.
bḥś to hunt.
bẖn (*bẖnw*) house.
bšy to be sick, to be soiled.
bšṯ to revolt.
btꜣw evil, squalor.
bdš become discouraged, to retreat.
bd·t (*bd·ty*) wheat, barley.

p

pꜣ to fly.
pꜣ-wn for, because.
pꜣw·t beginning.
pꜣw·ty cycle (of the gods).
pꜣw·t nṯrw cycle of the gods, nine-fold gods.
pꜣ-nty anyone.
pꜣ-śmy because of.
pᶜ·t tribe.
pwy demonstr. this.
pfś (*fśy*) to boil, to cook.
pnᶜ to upset, to turn around.
pry to go out, to ascend; hero.
pr-ᶜꜣ pharaoh.
pr-ffy an unknown place.
pr-ḥḏ treasury, double white house.
pr·ṯ Spring; grain.
pr·t-r-ẖrw funeral offerings.
pḥ to reach.
pḥwy hinder-part.
pḥ·ty strength, energy.
pẖr to penetrate.
pẖr·t remedy; troops.
pśy (*fśy*) to bake, to boil.
pśš to divide.
pśḏ back.
pśḏ·t the nine-fold gods.
pḳ·t fine linen.
p·t heaven.
ptny proper name.
ptr to see, to watch, to behold.
ptr (*pty*) what?
pḏ·t pśḏ the nine-bow people.

f

fꜣy to bring to, to give to, to carry, to take up, to start.
fy old abs. pron.
fnḏ nose, nostril.
fḫ to set forth.
fśy to cook, to bake, to boil.

m

m in, with, against.
mꜣᶜ (?) to slaughter, to offer (sacrifice).
mꜣᶜś·t liver (?).
mꜣᶜ·t truth, justly.
mꜣᶜ·t-kꜣ-rᶜ Hatshepsut.
mꜣwy to renew.
mꜣwṯ red granite.
mꜣḥ garland.
mꜣ-ḥsꜣ (*mꜣ-ḥs*) lion.
mꜣᶜ-ẖrw to justify, blessed, justified.
mꜣẖ to burn.
my like, as, that, when.
my (*mᶜy*) come!
myny to die.
my-śẖrw-n like, in the condition of.
my-ḳy after the manner of the whole.
my-ḳd like, quite.
mytt then.

mᶜ by, from, with, because, then, behold; for emphasis.
mᶜyw hair.
mᶜbꜣ 30
mᶜhry·t (*mẖry·t*) granary.
mᶜḥᶜ·t tomb.
mᶜt (*mṯ*) behold.
mw (*myw*) water.
mwt to die, to perish, to kill, the dead.
mw·t mother.
m-bꜣḥ before, in the presence of.
m-m (*mᶜ-mᶜ*) among.
m-mᶜ with, together with.
m-myt·t likewise, as well as.
m-mn·t daily.
mn to remain.
mn (*myny*) to be sick, to die, to land.
mny (*myny*) to die, to land, to rest, to depend; to marry.
mn-yb brave.
mny·t castanets.
mnᶜ·t nurse.
mnw monument.
mnw god Min.
mnw·t dove.
mnfy·t army, staff.
mnmn to quake.
mnmn·t herd.
mnḫ to be pleasant, to be favourable, excellent.
mn-ḫpr-rᶜ Thutmose III.
mnḫ·t linen, clothes.
mn·t anything.
mntw·f it, he.
mnṯw god Mont.
m-n-ḏrw when.
mr to grieve, to be anxious, to have pity for, grief, sorrowful; master, overseer, director, general; woman (?); canal; pyramid.
m-rꜣ-ᶜ nevertheless, as though.
mry to love, to desire, beloved.
mry·t river-bank.
m-rᶜ-ḫr but.
mrw-ynśy name of a man.
m-r-pw or.
mrmyptw name of a person.
mrḥ·t oil.
mr·t serving man.
mḥ to fill, to begin; ell.
m-ḥꜣ·t before.
mḥꜣ·t door.
m-ḥr-n to.
mḥ·ty north, northward.
m-ḫt after, afterwards, hereafter, behind, together.
m-ḫd northward.
m-ẖnw in, into, within, among, thereon.
m-ẖr·t-hrw daily.
msḥ crocodile.
mś child; for emphasis.
m-śꜣ after, behind, with.
mśy to give birth to, to be born.
mśy·t supper.
mśw·t childbirth.
mśḫn·t goddess of birth.
mśḏy to hate.
m·śḏm·t paint, black paint.
mšᶜ to walk, soldier, army.
mšw dagger.
m-ḳꜣb among, in the midst of.
mk lest.
mk (*mᶜk*) behold.
mky (*mᶜky*) to protect.
m-grg falsley.
mt- conjunctive prefix.
mty director.
mtw- conjunctive prefix.
mtw·k thou.
mtw·tw one, it; when.

m·tn behold (ye).
mtr to bear witness.
mṯ3 to defy.
mṯn (*mʿṯn*) way.
m-dy from.
mdw to speak, to cry, word, voice; staff of authority, authority.
mdnyt name of a place.
md·t word, matter.
m-ḏr because of.
m-ḏrty when.

n

n of, to, by (in swearing); not.
n3y·f his.
ny to belong to (*ny-śy mr-pr* it belongs to the master of the house).
nyw·ty·t (*nyw·ty*, *nyw·tt*) not, no, that which does not exist, not having.
nyś (*nysbḏ* [?]) to call, to proclaim.
n-ʿ3·t-n because.
nʿy to journey, to sail.
nʿr a kind of fish.
nw to see, to look; time; axe.
nwy to care for; flood; knife.
n-wr-n because of.
nw·t goddess Nut; town, city, residence.
nb each; gold; lord.
nb-m3ʿ·t-rʿ Amenophis III.
nb-k3w-rʿ name of a king.
nb·t lady.
nb·ty (?) "the two goddesses of the land," title of a king.
nbt-ḥt goddess Nephthys.
nbd to plait hair, lock of hair.
n-p3 but.
nfw (*ṯ3w*) breath; *nfrw* grain
nfr good; beauty; breath; *nfrw* grain.
nfry·t-r until.
nm (*nym*) who.
nmy to low, to shout.
nmyw-šʿyw name of nomads.
nmw payment.
nmḥ weak.
nmt to wander, wandering.
nn this, those.
n-nym-try who.
nry to fear.
nrw strength.
nrr to bow (?).
nr·t mankind.
nhw to despair; anything.
nhm to rejoice.
nhrn Naharína (Mesopotamia).
nhśy Nubian, negro.
nḥb·t neck.
nḥm to deliver, to escape, to take away, to rob.
nḥḥ for ever.
nẖw·t lamentation.
nẖb·t Nekhbet, name of a king; colour (?).
nẖn to be young; town Nechen.
nẖt to be strong, to be mighty, strength; victory.
nẖty name of a man.
nswy·t (?) kingdom.
nswt (?) king.
nś to belong to, according to measure.
nś·t throne.
nś·t-t3·wy Karnak.
nš to tremble; portal (?), step (?).
nkt thing.
ng3w bull; town of Nagau.
n·t city, town.
nty·t that which is, being, thing.
ntf it.
nt-ḥtr cavalry.
nṯr god.

nṯry divinity, divine.

nṯry·t godly, divinity.

nṯr nfr "good god" = the king.

nṯ-ḥtr charioteer.

nṯr·t goddess.

ndw to deliver, to set free.

nḏ to avenge.

nḏy·t pettiness.

nḏm to be sweet, to be glad, to please, to be well, to rejoice; sweet.

nḏnḏ to ask, to discourse.

nḏry to seize.

nḏ-ḥr homage.

nḏś to be small, little one.

n-ḏrtw when.

r to, since.

rꜣ mouth, voice, entrance, to talk; charm.

rꜣ-ꜣw a place-Tura.

rꜣ-yt door.

rꜣ-ꜥwy work.

r-ꜣw (*n-ꜣw*) throughout.

rꜣ-pw or.

rꜣ-pr temple.

rꜣ-ḥḏ treasure-house.

rꜣ-śṯꜣ-w Sakkara.

rꜥ day; the god Reꜥ.

rꜥ-wśr Wsr-rꜥ, name of a man.

rꜥ-bꜣk work.

rꜥ-ḥr-ꜣḫty Harmakhis.

r-ꜥḳꜣ opposite.

rwyy to flee, to escape.

rwy·t side.

rwhꜣ evening.

rwty double gate.

rpꜥ·t (*rpꜥ·ty*) prince, heir-apparent.

rf for emphasis.

rm fish.

rmy to weep.

r-my·ty·t in like manner.

rmn shoulder, arm, side.

rmṯ mankind.

rn name.

rnpy·t fruit, flowers.

rnp·t fruit; year.

rnn to suckle, to bring up.

r-nty·t introduces a final clause.

rḫ to know, to be learned, wisdom.

rḫy·t mankind, people.

r-ḫft before.

rḫty laundryman.

rś south.

rśy southern.

ršw to rejoice.

ršw·t joy.

ršrš to be glad, to be pleased, to enjoy.

rk time.

r-gś near, by the side of.

r-tw place (?).

rd to grow up, to develop; foot, leg.

rdy to give.

rdḏdt name of a woman.

r-ḏr whole.

r-ḏd that, introduces a final clause.

h

hꜣ hail!

hꜣy to go away, to advance, to descend, to pour in, to overthrow, to embark; husband.

hꜣw near; Oh!

hꜣb to send.

hy to rejoice; husband.

hb to labour.

hp law.

hmy to be ignorant.

hnw to shout for joy; pots.

hry to be satisfied.

hrw to be content; day.

hd hero.

hdhd to attack.

ḥ

ḥꜣ Oh!; behold.

ḥꜣ (*n-ḥꜣ*) behind.

ḥꜣw naked.

ḥꜣw-nb foreign countries.

ḥ(*ꜣ*)*pw·ty* spy.

ḥꜣ-ny Oh, that (in respect to me).

ḥꜣḳ to seize.

ḥꜣty heart.

ḥꜣ·ty before.

ḥꜣty-ꜥ beginning.

ḥꜣ·ty-ꜥ count, prince.

ḥꜣ·t-sp year of reign.

ḥꜥ flesh, body, limb.

ḥꜥy to rejoice.

ḥꜥw staff.

ḥꜥpy Nile.

ḥꜥt bed.

ḥw nourishment.

ḥwꜣ to be spoiled, to stink, to be annoyed.

ḥwy to smite, to beat, to pursue; Oh!

ḥwy·t rain.

ḥwn-n-n-nswt Herakleopolis.

ḥwtf to despoil.

ḥb to lament over (?), feast.

ḥbꜣbꜣ to waddle (of a goose).

ḥbś linen, garment, clothes.

ḥpt the arms.

ḥfꜣw snake, dragon.

ḥm male-servant; majesty.

ḥmꜣy·t salt.

ḥmw poor; rudder; 40.

ḥmw·t workshops.

ḥmw·ty workmen.

ḥm-nṯr prophet, priest.

ḥmśy to sit, to set, to place; sitting.

ḥm-kꜣ priest of the dead.

ḥm·t woman, wife, lady.

ḥn (*ḥnnw*) to go; to bar.

ḥnw goods, property; vase, jar.

ḥnw·t lady.

ḥnwty farmer.

ḥnwtt name of a lady.

ḥnmm·t mankind, people.

ḥnn (*ḥnnw*) phallus.

ḥnś narrow.

ḥnky·t bed.

ḥnk·t gift.

ḥr upon, to, because; overseer; Horus.

ḥry withdrawn; chief; name of a person.

ḥry-yb dwelling in.

ḥry·w-šꜥ sand-dwellers.

ḥry·t terror; the upper.

ḥry-tp chief.

ḥry-ḏꜣḏꜣ chief.

ḥrw upper path.

ḥrw-r except, in addition to.

ḥr-m why!

ḥr-mꜥ in front of.

ḥr-nhw-n for the sake of.

ḥr-ntt because, as it is.

ḥrr·t flower.

ḥr-śꜣ after.

ḥr-śhm·t-rꜥ-ꜥnḫ name of a king.

ḥr·t grave, necropolis.

ḥḥ for ever; million.

ḥs to arrive.

ḥsy to praise; praiseworthy; singing.

ḥsw·t favour, love, honour.

ḥsmn natron.

ḥs·t praise, favour.

ḥśy to sing, singer; an offering.

ḥśb to reckon; measures.
ḥśḳ to cut off.
ḥḳꜣ prince, ruler.
ḥḳꜣ·t lordship.
ḥḳr hungry.
ḥḳ·t beer, ale; goddess Ḥeḳt.
ḥkꜣ (in plural) magic.
ḥknw praise, thanksgiving.
ḥkr hungry.
ḥ·t fortress, castle, wall.
ḥtp to rest, to sit down, to set free, to satisfy; a measure, basket; offering.
ḥtp-dy-nswt an offering which the king gives.
ḥtpw-nṯr offering, oblation.
ḥtp-nfr-ḥk-wꜣś·t-ymn Amenophis II.
ḥtp-ḥk-wꜣś·t-ymn Amenophis III.
ḥtp·t food, offerings.
ḥtm to cease, to go to ruins.
ḥ·t-nṯr temple.
ḥtr team, cavalry.
ḥ·t-ḥr Hathor.
ḥtt shameful deed.
ḥdb to arrive, to pass time.
ḥd·t white crown, crown of Upper Egypt.
ḥḏ to be bright, white, silver.
ḥḏy to be unusable.
ḥḏ·t white crown of Upper Egypt.
ḥḏ-tꜣ the earth becomes bright = sunrise.

ḫ

ḫꜣ 1000.
ḫꜣy·t slaughter.
ḫꜣʿ to fall, to throw, to leave.
ḫꜣwy night.
ḫꜣw·t altar.
ḫꜣrw Syria.
ḫꜣr·t widow.
ḫꜣś·t foreign land, desert, land, bank.
ḫꜣś·ty foreigner, Bedouin.
ḫʿy to shine, to adorn.
ḫʿw shining, splendour; crown; tools; weapon, javelin.
ḫʿw-nw-rꜣ-ʿ-ḫt weapons.
ḫʿr to rage.
ḫʿ-kꜣ·w-rʿ Sesostris III.
ḫwś to build.
ḫbꜣ to ill-treat.
ḫby to dance.
ḫbśw·t (*ḫbsw·t*) beard.
ḫpy·t death.
ḫpr to come into being; a figure.
ḫpry sun-god.
ḫprw forms, being.
ḫpš strength.
ḫft to, before, just as, according to.
ḫfty enemy.
ḫft-ḥr before, in the presence of.
ḫm (*šmm*) to be hot, dry.
ḫmy not to do, not to know, to loose consciousness.
ḫmt to propose, to think.
ḫmt third.
ḫn to dance.
ḫnw·t musician.
ḫnmś friend, friendship.
ḫnm·t waiting women.
ḫn-n-md·t speech, discourse, proverb.
ḫnr (*ḫny*) prisoner.
ḫnr·t (?) prison.
ḫnt forehead.
ḫnty to journey southward, southward; first.

ḫnty-ymn·tyw "First of the Westerners" = a title of Osiris as god of the dead.

ḫnd to tread; throne.

ḫndw throne.

ḫr to fall; hostile prince; and, but; among, near, with, when, then, until.

ḫry belonging to.

ḫr-yr now, when, yet.

ḫr-yr-ḥr when, after.

ḫrw voice, sound; army.

ḫrp to bring, to conduct, to advance; stela, tombstone.

ḫrpw mallet.

ḫr-n for.

ḫr-rʿ when.

ḫr-św-m Oh!

ḫr·t thing belonging to.

ḫrtw "they say."

ḫḫ neck, throat.

ḫsf to protect, to draw near.

ḫsḏ to mould.

ḫśbḏ lapis-lazuli.

ḫśf to drive away, to defend, to prosecute.

ḫt tree.

ḫ·t thing.

ḫtꜣ Ḫeta, Hittite country.

ḫty to inscribe.

ḫtf according as.

ḫtm to close, to lock, to seal; seal.

ḫdy to sail down stream, northward.

ẖ

ẖꜣb·t "wire" of the crown.

ẖꜣr a bin.

ẖpꜣ umbilical cord.

ẖmʿ to fall upon.

ẖmś to bend.

ẖn to enter into.

ẖny·t sailor.

ẖnw inside; abode, residence, palace.

ẖnw-ʿ to embrace, in arms.

ẖnm to unite oneself.

ẖnmw god Khnum.

ẖnm·t-ḥꜣ·t-špś·wt-ymn Hatshepsut.

ẖr under, with.

ẖry·t possession.

ẖry·t-nṯr underworld.

ẖr-ḥꜣ at the head of.

ẖr-ḥꜣ·t before, old time.

ẖrd child.

ẖsy to be weak, to be faint, miserable, despised, wretched.

ẖsy·t despised.

ẖ·t body, belly; people.

ẖdb to slay.

ẖdr misery (?).

s

s (*ꜣ* ?) man.

sꜣ son; priesthood.

sꜣw to beware, guardian; Nḫn, title of an official.

sꜣb jackal; judge.

sꜣnht Sinuhe.

sꜣ·t daughter.

sꜣṯ (*sꜣt*) to froth over.

s·ʿḳ to cause to go.

swnw name of a place.

swn·t sale.

swr (*swy*) to drink.

sb (*sby*) to go, to pass by, to follow.

sp time, example.

spꜣ·t district.

spy to remain over.

sp-pw is it the time?, is it worth while?

sf to be gracious.

sf·t (*sfṯ*) knife.

smꜣy to unite.

smꜣ-tꜣ neck or strip of land.

smy tidings.

smy·t desert.

sny to open, to spread out.

snf blood.
shs (*śḫśḫ*) to run.
sḫr leadership.
sḫs (*śḫśḫ*) flight.
ssm horse.
sš to write, scribe, book, writing.
sš see *sny*.
sšn blossom of the lotus.
sšš·t sistrum.
s·t woman.
sd tail.

ś

ś3 back.
ś33 to recognize.
ś3y to satisfy; fierce-eyed.
ś3b judge.
ś3r woe.
ś3ḥ to reach, to approach, to present with.
ś3ẖbw proper name.
ś3ḳ to gather together.
śy3ḫ to glorify.
śyny to await.
śᶜb trinkets.
śᶜḥ nobility, freedom.
św the sun, light.
św3y to pass, to go by.
św3ḥ to continue.
św3š to worship, to praise.
śwḥ·t egg.
śwt (= *św*) 3 per. mas. sing. per. pron.
śwḏ to inherit, to provision.
śwḏ to command.
śwḏ3 to refresh, to give health to.
śb3 door.
śbḥ to laugh, to cry, to call out.
śbk god Sebek.
śpr to come, to go, to arrive, to reach; to bewail, to lament, lamentation.
śpry to let go forth.
śpdd to make ready, to be.
śf yesterday.
śm (*śmw*, *śtmw*) vegetables.
śm3 to kill, to do battle.
śm3ᶜ to pray, to cry; forehead.
śm3ᶜ to justify.
śmy to report; because of.
śmwn truly.
śmn goose.
ś·mnḫ to beautify.
śmr friend, companion.
śmḥy left, east.
śn brother.
śny to curse.
śnw to complain.
śnb to be well, health.
śn-nw a second, a companion.
śnḫbḫb to draw back (?).
śn·t sister.
śn·ty both sisters.
śnṯr incense.
śnḏ to be afraid, fear.
śnḏ3r3 country of Sendar.
śnḏm to dwell, to sit.
śr (*śyr*) prince, high official, burgher, princely.
śrw princes.
śrḫ throne.
śrḫy to announce to.
śḥw to assemble.
śḥry to take oneself away.
śḥtm to destroy.
śḥḏ to make bright, to clear up, to manifest.
śḫ3 to remember, to bethink, to think.
śḫ3ḫ to assist, to hasten.
śḫpr to cause to exist.
śḫm to be powerful, might; double crown, sceptre.

śḫr to overthrow; counsel, manner, nature, thing; according to the manner of, according to.

śḫśḫ to run, to pursue.

śḫ·t field.

śḫ·ty peasant, fellah, farmer.

śḫd stand on head, upside down.

śẖr to overlay.

śẖ·ty peasant.

śšpd to be in good order.

śšm·t a mare.

śšn to smell, to breathe.

śšm to lead, to fashion (?).

śšmw guide, leader, fashioner.

śšt3 to enchant.

śšd diadem.

śḳbbwy bath-room.

śḳr-ᶜnḫ prisoner.

śḳd rower.

śḳdy to sail.

śk behold.

śk3 to plough.

śkm to finish.

śkśk to destroy.

śgnn ointment.

śgr silence.

ś·t (*yś·t*) place.

śt3 to lift, to take away; to make light, fire.

śty to discharge a bow; Nubia; smell.

śtyw (*śṯtyw*) Asiatics, bedouin.

ś·t-yry right place, in (their season).

ś·t-wr·t throne.

śtp to choose.

śtpw the best, the choise.

śṯ when.

śṯ3 to lead.

śṯp to choose.

śṯp·t oblation, offering of flesh.

śṯ·ty Syrian.

śd to clothe; tail.

śḏf3 to supply with, supply.

śḏm to hear.

śḏr to lie down, to sleep, to spend the night.

š

š pond.

š3 tree, garden.

š3ᶜ-m since.

š3w weight, quantity.

š3b victuals.

š3ś to go, to hasten.

š3śy to go.

š3·t-dw3 150.

š3d to dig.

šᶜ (*šᶜy*) sand.

šᶜ·t book.

šᶜd to cut, cut off, cut down.

šw sun.

šw3 common man, poor man.

šwy to be dry.

šwy-m empty = without.

šw·ty double feather (king's crown).

špś monument, stela.

špśy holy, fine; Sacred Lady, Principal Favourite.

špśś wealth.

šfy·t strength.

šm to go.

šmy to go.

šmᶜ south; dancing.

šmᶜy·t dancing girl.

šmᶜ-sp·t district of Upper Egypt.

šmw wheat.

šmm to be hot, to be dry.

šmśy to serve, to follow.

šmśw follower, servant, bodyguard; following.

šmś-ḥr servants of Horus, Kings of antiquity.

šn to be sick, to be grieved, to suffer.
šny to encircle.
šny (*šnw*) hair.
šnʿ to avert; edge of a path.
šnw·t courtiers.
šnb·t skin, body.
šnḏw·t skirt, clothing.
šry small, younger (of persons).
šry·t young person; daughter.
šś linen.
šsp to receive, to take, to begin, to conceive; statue of a god.
šś wardrobe; alabaster.
šś3 ability.
šdy to read; to suckle.

ḳ

ḳ3y to leap; to raise.
ḳ3y·t high.
ḳ3ḳ3w a ship.
ḳ3g3b name of a man.
ḳy fulness.
ḳby to increase.
ḳbb to be cool, to refresh.
ḳm3 to create; form, figure, person.
ḳmy ointment, salve.
ḳmʿtw southern.
ḳn to be many, many.
ḳny to be strong, to be brave, to carry; porter.
ḳny·t strength.
ḳnḳn to beat.
ḳn·t domain.
ḳnd rage.
ḳnd·t rage.
ḳry thunder.
ḳrśw coffin.
ḳr·t (?) bolt.
ḳś to be sick; bone.
ḳśn foolish.
ḳḳ3 to rule over.
ḳd to build; figure, likeness, character; like.
ḳdy to walk.
ḳdnwm name of a place.
ḳdtr dirty.

k

k3 soul (" Ka "); bull; behold, verily, in truth.
k3y to speak, to say aloud, to think, to desire, to plan, to forsee.
k3wty workman.
k3-nḫt-ḫʿ-m-w3ś·t Thutmose III.
k3ry Nubian country.
k3š Kush.
k3·t work; wife, woman.
k3tw hidden.
ky (*kyy*) another.
kwkw darkness.
kw·ty thou.
kf3 to uncover.
km to finish.
km·t Egypt.
kśy to bow.
kśw crouched position.
kš Nubia.
kšt Kush.
kkw darkness.
kty another.
kty-yḫ·t another matter, others.
ktkt to twitch.
kdšw Kadesh.

g

g3y vase, vessel.
g3š3 grief.
gb (*gbb*) god Geb.
gb3 arm, side.
gbgb to cast down, to fall.
gmy to find.
gmḥ to see, to perceive.
gmḥ·t crown.
gmgm to creek.
gnn (*g3nn*) to be weak, helpless.
gr to be silent.

grḥ to rest, to be calm.
grg to found, to build, to take, to provide for, to lay a trap.
grg faithless, false; baseness, falsehood.
gr·t but.
gś side, half; to anoint, to perfume.
gšy dagger.

t

tꜣ bread, earth.
tꜣ-wnw·t at once.
tꜣ-mry Egypt.
tꜣš border, frontier.
tꜣ-ḏśr cemetery.
tyy Queen Tiy.
tyw yes.
tywy belonging to thee.
ty-rꜣ-yꜣ door.
tw- late Egyptian prefix.
tw "one," thou, thee.
twt image, statue; unite, be together.
tp head, first.
tpy first, beginning, chief; to breathe.
tpy-ʿ ancestor.
tpy·t fine oil.
tp-ʿ before.
tp-m before.
tp-ḥśb exactness.
tpty fine oil, fine.
tf (*yt*) father.
tm to stop, not to do.
tm (see *ytm*).
tmyt lest.
tny old age.
tnw name of a place, Tnw = Rtnw (?).
tnnw each; weakness (?).
tr (*ty*) time.
try pray! to mark a question.
tr-n during, while.
thy to err, to transgress, to attack.
thmy (*thy*) to drive out.
thn to proclaim.
tḫn obelisk.
tkn to consort with.
tty King Tety.

ṯ

ṯꜣ chicken.
ṯꜣy to seize, to shave; man, male.
ṯꜣw wind (see *nfw*).
ṯꜣ·ty vizier.
ṯʿw to run.
ṯwyꜣ mother of Queen Tiy.
ṯb vessel.
ṯb·t sandal.
ṯpḥ·t cavern.
ṯny sheikh (?); town This; Thinis district.
ṯnrʿ mighty deeds.
ṯnṯꜣ·t throne.
ṯḥwḥw to rejoice.
ṯḫn to draw nigh, to collide.
ṯs proverb.
ṯsy to raise, to lift up, to exalt.
ṯsw to command, a general.
ṯtw (*ṯb·t*) sandals.

d

d (*dy*) to put; here; there.
dꜣy (*dꜣr*) to rule.
dꜣb fig.
dy to give; *dy-ʿnḫ* "given life."
dwꜣ to adore, to praise, to instruct (?), to become morning; early, to-morrow.
dwꜣy·t morning.
dwn to throw down, to lie down, to stretch out.
dbꜣ to give back.
dbn to search.
dbḥ to beseech.
dp bushel.
dp·t ship, boat; taste.

df drop (?).
dm to sharpen; to name.
dmy to arrive at, to come after, to be related to; city, town, village, place.
dmy·t city.
dm·t knife.
dny to take part.
dr to vanquish, to destroy, to drive away.
drp to present, to make libation, to offer sacrifice.
dhny to name.
dḥwty god Thot.
dḥr leather.
dśr grave.
dḳr fruit.
d·t hand.
ddy Dedy (a person).
ddwn Dedwn (a person).

ḏ

ḏꜣy to cross, to cross the water.
ḏꜣmw generation.
ḏꜣḏꜣ head; college of priests.
ḏꜣḏꜣ-m to.
ḏꜣḏꜣ·t college.
ḏꜥ storm.
ḏꜥm gold.
ḏw mountain; evil (*ḏw·t*).
ḏbꜣ to stop, to pay, payment, wages.
ḏbꜥ·t seal.
ḏb·t brick, tile.
ḏfꜣ food.
ḏr extremity, whole; since.
ḏrw boundary, limit.
ḏr·t hand.
ḏḥwty god Thot.
ḏḥwty-mś-nfr-ḫprw Thutmose III.
ḏḥwty-nḫt proper name.
ḏśr-mnw-ymn name of a door.
ḏśr-kꜣ-rꜥ Amenophis I.
ḏ·t eternity, for ever; serf.
ḏd to speak; to last; account.
ḏdw city Busiris.
ḏdb to collect.
ḏd·t endurance, duration, stability.